GO-AHEAD RIDER

GO-AHEAD RIDER

ROBERT J. CONLEY

M. EVANS AND COMPANY, INC.   NEW YORK

Library of Congress Cataloging-in-Publication Data

Conley, Robert J.

Go-ahead Rider / Robert J. Conley.
    p.   cm. — (An Evans novel of the West)
  ISBN 0-87131-612-9 : 15.95
  I. Title.   II. Series.
PS3553.0494G64   1990
813'.54—dc20

M. Evans and Company, Inc.
216 East 49 Street
New York, New York 10017

Manufactured in the United States of America

9 8 7 6 5 4 3 2 1

Chapter One

George Tanner wasn't prepared for the sights and sounds that greeted him in Tahlequah when he stepped off the stagecoach. The sidewalks of the small town were crowded with people jostling each other, and the streets were busy with the traffic of wagons, carts, and men on horseback, going, it seemed to George, in all directions at once. It reminded him of the traffic of the big eastern cities he had seen. And there in the square was a large, two-story brick building that had not been there four years earlier when he had left to go to college. He knew as soon as he saw it, though, that it was the new Cherokee National Capitol Building. They had been talking about it back then before he had left.

Then he realized that the Council must be in session. That was the only likely explanation for the extraordinary crowds of people in town. Council meetings had always drawn large crowds to Tahlequah, but this was the largest he had ever seen. At least he thought it was. His luggage was stacked there on the sidewalk in front of the Capital Hotel where the stage driver had dumped it, along with George, and he had to find someplace to stash it while he looked for a place to live.

The Civil War in Indian Territory had cost him his parents and his home, and his raising had been finished in the Cherokee Orphanage. Three years after the war had ended, George's education was finished as far as it could go in the Cherokee Nation, and Mr. Grant, the missionary, had made all the arrangements and had sent him to college at Harvard. Now, his college education completed, his new degree in the classics in hand, George Tanner had come home to the Cherokee Nation. He had come home, but he had no home. Since he had been deposited there in front of the Capital Hotel, he decided to try for a room. He went inside and found the proprietor there behind his counter.

"I'd like a room for the night," said George.

"You won't find anything in town," said the proprietor. "Haven't you seen the crowds out there? Everything's taken."

George was slightly taken aback. He couldn't think of where else to turn. The man, he thought, was probably right about there being no rooms available in town.

"Well," he said, "I just came in on the stage. I have some luggage out on the sidewalk. Can I leave it here?"

The proprietor scratched his head and looked around, looking as if he were searching for an excuse to say no. Not finding one, he answered with a shrug.

"I guess you could stash it here behind the counter," he said, "for a while."

"Thanks."

George lugged it inside and put it where the man indicated, then went back out onto Muskogee Avenue, the busy main street. He couldn't help but notice that a majority of the people in town had the appearance of white people, like the proprietor of the hotel and like—well, he thought, like me. He assumed that, also like himself, they were mostly mixed-blood citizens of the Cherokee Nation.

He needed to find a place to stay, and the prospects looked pretty dim. Even so, his curiosity pulled him toward the new capitol building. It was certainly the most impressive building in town, probably, George imagined, in the whole territory. He felt a surge of pride just standing there looking at it: the capitol building of the Cherokee Nation, his national capitol. The square on which the capitol stood was noticeably free of the wandering crowds, but George saw five armed guards on the square. Obviously their job was to keep the crowd away from the building while the Council was in session. He decided not to challenge them by seeing just how close he could get to the building before they would stop him, so he stood on the sidewalk across the street from the square to study the new edifice.

Then he heard a shot. It came from somewhere up on the north end of the street. There wasn't a whole lot up there. The Cherokee Male Seminary, the oldest institution of higher learning west of the Mississippi River, was up there at that end of the street, and there were a few small shops and some scattered residences, mostly small log cabins. George looked toward the sound just like everyone else did, and then there was another shot. A few souls, either brave or foolhardy but certainly curious, started to run in that direction. The rest, including George, craned their necks to see what they could see from their relatively safe positions. George felt a hand slap him on the back, and he turned his head. It was Captain Go-Ahead Rider, who had been a captain in the Indian Home Guard, U.S. Army, during the Civil War, and that was the only thing George had known about him. George had been just a youngster back then, but he had seen Rider and he'd heard people talk about him. Rider wasn't wearing a uniform anymore, though, and George saw that he had a star pinned on his vest.

"*Inena,*" Rider said, and he started to move on.

"What?" said George.

Rider hesitated and looked back.

"Don't you understand Cherokee?" he said. "Come with me. You're deputized."

George knew that a district sheriff of the Cherokee Nation could deputize any citizen when he needed help, and he knew that any citizen so deputized who refused to comply was subject to a fine. His funds were limited, and he still didn't have a place to live. Besides that, Go-Ahead Rider had been for several years a hero to George, so George followed him. Rider led George up toward the north end of the street and the edge of town, and there the crowd thinned out. Another shot was fired. George still couldn't tell just where the shots were coming from. Rider turned toward the curious few who had come up the street just about as far as he and George.

"Get on back down there now," he said. "Someone could get hurt here."

Another shot rang out, and the people turned and ran back down the street. Rider shot a quick glance toward George.

"You got a gun?" he asked.

"No, sir," said George.

In his belt Rider had two Navy Colts, and he pulled one out and handed it to George butt first. George took the gun and, feeling somewhat awkward and stupid, held it out in front of himself aimed at the ground about five feet away.

"Right up there," said Rider, pointing to a log cabin up the hill about a hundred yards from where they stood. "Jesse Halfbreed's in the house there, and back there behind, somewhere in them trees, is Tom Spike Buck. They're both drunk. I'd rather not shoot them, but shoot them before you let them shoot you."

"Yes, sir," said George.

"You go over there behind that big oak and watch the front of the house. I'll get Tom first. Then we'll worry about Jess."

Rider started out for the trees but not in a direct line. He made a wide circle so that he could slip up on Tom Spike Buck. George stood and watched him for a minute, looked at the cabin, and then ran straight for the big oak. He got safely behind the big tree, and then he peeked around it, but he had lost sight of Go-Ahead Rider. Rider must have already made it to the trees behind the cabin. George focused his eyes on the front door of the house as Rider had told him to, and he waited. Then he thought, My God, what if I have to shoot a man that I don't even know just because he's drunk and just because I happened to be standing there handy when Go-Ahead Rider needed a temporary deputy real fast? Of course, he remembered, Rider had said that he shouldn't shoot unless he had to. Still, he felt like he was in a pretty touchy situation.

Then it got quiet, real quiet, and George started to get nervous. He didn't know what was going on in either the house or back in the trees. He felt his palm begin to sweat against the butt of the Colt .36. Then he heard Rider call out from in the trees.

"Jess," he said. "This is Sheriff Rider. I just knocked Tom over the head, and he's out cold. Ain't nothing left for you to shoot at. Toss that gun out and come out of the house."

Another shot sounded, and George couldn't be sure from where he was posted, but he figured that Jess Halfbreed had fired out the back of the house at Rider. Then the front door flew open, and a man, Jesse Halfbreed, George guessed, came running out. He had a pistol in his hand, and he was running straight for the big oak that shielded George. Apparently he didn't see George, and thought that Rider was alone, and George was determined to keep it that way for as long as possible. He pressed himself against the trunk of the big oak and waited. He waited until he could hear the man's feet pounding the ground and knew that he was getting close. Then George peeked around the tree trunk. The runner was nearly on him, but he had just looked back over his shoulder and hadn't seen George peer around the tree. It looked to George as if the man intended to race right past the tree and keep going. Just as he was about to pass the oak, George stepped out and stuck a foot in his path. The fugitive went sprawling facedown on the ground. He lost his grip on his pistol, and it flew out beyond his reach. He looked up and saw George, then he started to scramble forward after his lost weapon, but George stepped up quickly and set down a foot hard on the man's hand, the one that was reaching for the gun. He aimed the Navy Colt at the man's head and thumbed back the hammer.

"Just be still," he said. "I sure don't want to kill you."

"I'm sick," said the captive, but he relaxed, and George moved forward to pick up the gun he had dropped, an old Remington .44. He tucked it in the waistband of his trousers and stepped back beyond the other man's reach. Then he looked off toward the trees. Rider was dragging a limp body out into the open. He looked up to see George and waved at him to come over.

"Get up," George said, and he marched his prisoner over to the sheriff.

"You watch these two," said Rider. "I'll be back."

Rider walked back down onto Muskogee Avenue and approached a man in a wagon. Pretty soon he climbed up on the wagon seat beside the driver, and the man drove his wagon up to where George was waiting. They loaded the two prisoners into the wagon and drove them to the jail, a small stone building just south of the capitol. When Rider had locked up the prisoners, he took George into his office and offered him a cup of coffee. George accepted. Rider handed him the coffee, and George returned the Navy Colt to Rider and gave him Jesse Halfbreed's Remington.

"Sit down," said Rider.

George sat and sipped at the hot coffee.

"I owe you a dollar for that job," said Rider. "I have to put in a request for it, but you'll get it. I'm Go-Ahead Rider."

He stuck out his right hand, and George took it in his.

"I know who you are," said George. "I didn't know you were sheriff, though. Not until just now."

"I was appointed sheriff of Tahlequah District about a year ago," said Rider.

"I've been away," said George, "to school. I've been gone four years."

"You're the Tanner boy, ain't you?" said Rider. "From Park Hill?"

"Yes, sir. George Tanner. You know me.?"

"I knew your father. He was a good man."

"Yes, sir."

6

George Tanner felt just a bit pumped up inside, finding out that Go-Ahead Rider knew who he was. Rider had been famous among the Indians since George's childhood, and not just among the Cherokees. He was known throughout Indian Territory, Arkansas, Missouri, and Kansas. And he had recognized George, and that made George feel proud.

"I saw you get off the stage," said Rider, "and when Jess Halfbreed's wife came to get me and said there was trouble up at her house, I decided to try you out."

"You've got five deputies out there," said George.

"And I want to keep them out there. They're temporary help hired for the duration of the Council meeting to keep order around the capitol building. There's a bunch of folks in town and some hot issues before the council."

Rider stopped talking and opened up a desk drawer from which he took out a corncob pipe and a tobacco pouch. He filled the pipe, struck a wooden match on the side of his desk, and lit the tobacco.

"What are your plans, George?" he said.

"I don't know. I just got back from college. I guess I'll look for a job of some kind. As soon as I find a place to live. There don't seem to be any rooms in town, and my old home place is gone. Burned during the war."

"Yeah, I know," said Rider. He puffed on his pipe. He was leaning back in his chair, his feet propped on a corner of his desk. He wore high, black leather boots with his trouser legs tucked into them. His two .36-caliber Navy Colts, retooled to accept bullets instead of balls and black powder, which he had previously carried in the waistband of his trousers behind his wide, black belt, were lying on the desk in front of him. His black vest, on which his star was pinned, was hanging open, the two sides connected only by a gold watch chain, and under the vest he wore a loose-fitting, white cotton shirt. His coal-black hair grew to his shoulders, and the white smoke from his pipe, which seemed to hover momentarily in wisps around his head before it slowly rose and dissipated, only served to set off by stark contrast his dark brown skin. He wore a thin mustache, the ends of which grew down past the corners of his mouth. His eyes were nearly black and his features finely chiseled. He seemed to George Tanner almost a perfect picture of the war hero or the fighting frontier lawman.

"I need a full-time deputy," Rider said finally. "Permanent. You want the job?"

George's face registered surprise. He looked at Rider, then quickly looked back down at the cup he held in his hands. Staring into another's eyes was not considered polite among the Cherokees. Staring too long and hard was even considered threatening.

"I don't know," he said. "I never thought about being a lawman."

"What did you study in college?" said Rider.

"The classics. You know, Greek and Latin."

"Mmm," said Rider. "Where did you go? What school, I mean."

"Harvard."

"I like the way you handled yourself out there just now with old Jess," said Rider.

"Thank you."

"So what do you say?"

George stood up and paced the floor. He did need a job, and he needed a place to stay. He had been offered a teaching position back east when he had graduated, but the idea of teaching just hadn't appealed to him. Besides that, he had wanted to go home. But a deputy sheriff? He turned back to face Go-Ahead Rider, who sat calmly smoking his pipe.

"Why me?" said George.

"I liked your father."

"I just don't know. I never handled guns much. I did box and wrestle in college. I don't know, Captain Rider."

"Well," said Rider, "let's go get your bags and put them up at my house. You'll stay with me for tonight. You can think about the job and give me an answer in the morning. If you decide you want to try it out, we'll make it temporary. Give it a month to kind of try each other out. Come on."

* * *

That evening they were all gathered around the table in Go-Ahead Rider's home: George Tanner, Rider, Rider's wife, Exie, and the two Rider children, Tootie, a nine-year-old girl, and Buster, a five-year-old boy. Rider said a prayer in Cherokee, and then they all dug in. They had catfish and dumplings and sweet corn and greens. The Riders spoke only Cherokee at home. Tootie was learning English at school and could speak some, but little Buster knew only Cherokee. Exie could understand English but couldn't—or wouldn't—speak it. George's Cherokee was not quite as good as Exie's English. He understood some. It had been four years since George had even heard Cherokee spoken, and the language sounded good to his ears. When the meal was finished, George leaned back in his chair from the table.

"*Wado,*" he said. He did know how to say "thank you" in Cherokee. "That was real good."

Exie smiled and said something back to him which he couldn't quite make out. He looked at her for a moment, and then he glanced at Rider.

"Did you have enough?" said Rider.

"Oh. Oh, yeah," said George. "Plenty. I'm full. Stuffed."

Exie moved back to the table with the coffeepot in her hand. She poured her husband's cup full, then turned to George.

"*Kawi jaduli?*" she said.

"Yes," said George. "I could take some more coffee. *Wado.*"

When Exie had filled George's cup, Rider stood up, his cup in hand.

"Lets go outside," he said.

George picked up his cup and followed Rider out. Rider had two log cabins built no more than twelve or fourteen feet apart. The space between the cabins was paved with flat stones and fenced in on both sides with a low picket fence. It was to some chairs and small tables in this "dog run" that Rider led George. They sat down in the pleasant evening air and looked over Tahlequah. Rider's home was built up on the high bluff east of town so that they looked down at the back side of the new capitol building. The town looked quiet enough. They could see only a few people still milling around the streets.

"Captain Rider," said George, "—or maybe I should call you Sheriff Rider now."

"I get called both ways," said Rider. "Call me what you like."

"What are the big issues before the Council that drew so many people to town?"

"Main thing is the railroad issue. You know we had to let the railroad go through by the treaty we signed after the Civil War. They just recently got it finished on down to Texas."

"Yeah," said George. "I rode it to Muskogee coming home."

"There's some wanting to bring tracks right in here. Into Tahlequah," said Rider. "The Council's pretty well divided on the issue. The full-bloods is all against it. The mixed-bloods is mostly for it. Except for old Mix Hail. Mix is only about a quarter Cherokee, I guess, if that much, but he's lined up with the full-bloods on this issue. In fact, he's sort of their ring leader, and a couple of his friends, other mixed-blood council members, are kind of following him along. At least they're not committed one way or the other yet. The way the other side has it figured, the ones that want the railroad to come in here, if it wasn't for old Mix, they could pull them other two over to their side real easy and have it made."

George slurped some coffee, and he thought that it sure did taste good, drinking it out in the night air.

"Why does everyone care so much about the railroad coming in?" he asked.

"Railroads change everything, George. They bring all kinds of people in. Some say if the railroad comes in, gambling, liquor, prostitution and all kinds of crime is bound to follow. The ones who want it say it brings prosperity, progress, new business. I imagine they even got ways figured out where they can make a profit from it personally, at least some of them. Old Mix and the full-bloods, well, they want Tahlequah to stay like it is."

"What do you think?"

"I ain't paid to think, George, just to uphold the law."

George squinted at Rider in the dim light of the evening. Rider had declined to express an opinion on the railroad issue, yet George felt that Rider had already in an indirect way made his feelings known. George thought that Rider wouldn't like to see the railroad come into Tahlequah.

"Anyhow," Rider continued, "the council members is all in town, some with their families. Others just come in to be here while the Council's in session. Some are here because they care about the issues, I guess, and they want to be right here to learn about the decision just as soon as possible after it's made. Some just use the council session as a good excuse to come to town and have a party. Then there's some railroad people in town. They've hired a man named Omer Lyons, a mixed-blood citizen. His job, I think, is to try to convince the councilmen to vote for the railroad. Oh, yeah, because of all this activity, Elwood Lovely's in town, too."

"Who's he?" asked George.

"Deputy U.S. Marshal assigned to this part of the territory out of Fort Smith, Arkansas."

"You don't need him around, do you?" said George.

"I'm glad to have him," said Rider. "You know, I'm not allowed to arrest a white man. Not unless he's a Cherokee citizen."

"Rider," said George, and he felt suddenly bold addressing the man so familiarly. He had noticed at dinner that Exie called him Rider. Just Rider. Of course, she had said it in Cherokee, *Agiluh-disgoi*. And he was feeling good being back home. He was comfortable there with Rider and his family, and maybe, he thought, because he was an orphan with no home, he just wanted to find a family to belong to. Just then Tootie and Buster came running out of the house, and one jumped on one of Rider's knees and one on the other. They talked for a little while in Cherokee. George thought that he understood something about going to bed. Then they each kissed their father, and they ran back into the house.

"Rider," said George, "I think I'd like to try that job."

Chapter Two

They were up early the next morning, and after a big breakfast of eggs and sausage and biscuits and gravy cooked by Exie, they went down to the office in the jail. Jesse Halfbreed and Tom Spike Buck were asleep in their cells. Rider built up a little fire in the stove and put some coffee on to boil. George, figuring that he might easily wind up with that chore, watched closely. Then Rider sat down behind his desk, opened a drawer, and pulled out some papers.

"Got to do some paperwork on those boys we threw in yesterday," he said. "You might as well watch over my shoulder so you'll know how to do them. Now we got old Tom Spike Buck on drunk and disorderly, and we got him for carrying a weapon. Jess Halfbreed, we got him for drunk and disorderly, carrying a weapon—which we wouldn't have if he hadn't run out of his own house carrying that pistol—and we got him for resisting arrest."

He finished filling out the two forms and put them to one side. There were two remaining forms, different from the first ones.

"These here," he said to George, "I got to fill out on you. This one's to get your dollar from yesterday. This one's to employ you permanently."

When Rider had finished his paperwork, he checked the coffeepot and then poured two cups. When the two had finished their coffee, Rider picked up the paperwork from his desk.

"Come on," he said. "We have to go see the judge and the clerk."

When Rider and George reached the capitol building, the special deputies were already gathering. Rider called them all together there in front of the building.

"Boys," he said, "I want you to meet our new deputy sheriff. This is George Tanner. Some of you might remember Hickory and Modean over at Park Hill. George is their boy. He's just back from four years at Harvard."

Then he turned to George.

"George," he said, "these are all special deputies hired just for the council meeting, and they're all good men if you ever need a hand. Remember them. This is Elmer Lee, Brodie Hicks, Delbert Swim, Earl Bob, and Beehunter."

George shook hands with each man in turn while Rider kept talking.

"Beehunter don't talk English, so if you need to tell him anything, you have to talk Cherokee—or else get an interpreter."

Then he spoke for a short while in Cherokee to Beehunter. George guessed that he was telling Beehunter what he had already told the others in English. While that was going on, George noticed men in suits beginning to show up. Council members gathering for the meeting, he figured. Then Rider sent the special deputies to their posts.

"Come on," he said to George.

They walked up to the front door of the capitol and went inside, and Rider went over to an office door and opened it to peek inside.

He said something which George couldn't hear, then looked back at George.

"Come on in here a minute," he said.

George followed him inside the office, and there he saw a gaunt figure of a man dressed in an expensive suit. He was a very dignified-looking gentleman, with white hair and a long, white beard. He had pale, almost watery, blue eyes and a benign expression on his face. George thought that he looked like some kind of missionary.

"Sir," said Rider, "this is George Tanner, my new deputy. George, this is Principal Chief William P. Ross."

George hoped that the chief didn't notice his jaw drop. The chief extended a thin, white hand, and George took it.

"I'm pleased to meet you, Mr. Tanner," said Ross. "I hope the job works out well for you."

"Thank you, sir," said George.

Rider took their leave of the chief and led George back into the hall and up the stairs to the second floor. He gestured toward two large doors toward the back of the building.

"That's the council chambers," he said. Then he turned toward a small office at the front. "This is the judge's office. Come on."

They went inside and found the judge at his desk. When he saw the two men he stood up to greet them.

"Good morning, Go-Ahead," he said.

"Good morning, your honor. I'd like you to meet my new deputy, George Tanner. We're upgrading the sheriff's department. George is a Harvard graduate. This is Judge Boley, George."

"Harm Boley," said the judge, extending his hand for George to shake. "It's a pleasure."

"I'm pleased to meet you, sir," said George.

"We brought you a couple of arrest reports here," said Rider, and he handed Boley the forms he had filled out on his two prisoners. The judge glanced over the reports.

"Mmm," he said. "Jess again. This time it'll be a hundred lashes for him. Oh, well, some people never seem to learn."

He sat back down, checked a register, and filled out two small slips of paper, which he then handed to Rider. Rider tucked them into a vest pocket.

"Have you been to the clerk's office yet?" asked the judge.

"Not yet," said Rider. "That's our next stop."

"Drop this off there for me, would you please?" said Boley, handing Rider a large envelope.

"Be glad to."

They took their leave of the judge, and as they headed for the stairway, the sounds of the council meeting could be heard through the big doors. They went by the clerk's office, where George was introduced once more and Rider turned in the two papers on George and delivered the envelope from Judge Boley. Then they returned to the sheriff's office.

"Let's have one more cup of coffee and then get to work," said Rider.

"What do we do?" asked George.

"Well," said Rider, pouring coffee, "we arrested two drunks yesterday. Now we got to try to find out where they got their booze."

He handed a cup of coffee to George, poured himself one, and moved around behind his big desk. Then he motioned toward a smaller desk over in the corner of the room.

"That's yours," he said.

George went over to the desk and put his cup on it. He pulled out the chair and sat down. He put his hands on the wooden desk top and felt it. His desk. He liked it. Rider had reached down to pull open a bottom drawer of his desk. He took out a pistol in a holster, which was wrapped in a leather belt, and put it on top of his desk. He shut the drawer and opened another, from which he took out a badge. Then he stood up, picked up the gun and badge, and walked over to George's desk. He put the badge down on the desk in front of George.

"Pin that on," he said.

George stood up and picked up the badge. He held it in his hand for a moment and felt its slick surface, felt the star points, and then he pulled aside the left lapel of his suit coat and pinned the badge on his vest, just where Rider wore his. Rider put the pistol on George's desk.

"I tried this out once," he said. "It's the latest thing, but I guess I'm just too used to my old Colts. This is a Starr double-action Army .44."

"Double-action?" said George.

"You don't have to cock it. Just pull the trigger."

"Oh, yeah?"

"We'll go out sometime and let you try it out."

George pulled the Starr out of its holster and tucked it into the waistband of his trousers, the way Rider carried his Colts, but he found it to be too uncomfortable. He put it back in the holster and strapped on the belt. By the time he had done that, Rider was back behind his desk again. He opened up a drawer and called George's name. George looked up just in time to catch a box of .44 bullets Rider tossed at him.

"You might as well load that thing," said Rider. "And keep the shells. I don't use .44s."

George loaded five shells into the Starr and was about to put in a sixth.

"I'd leave that one empty," said Rider. "Always keep the hammer on an empty chamber for safety."

George carefully set the hammer on the empty chamber, holstered the Starr, and glanced over at Rider. Then he pulled off his suit coat and hung it on a coat tree that stood just inside the door. He made a mental note to get himself a pair of boots as soon as possible.

"You ready to go to work now?" said Rider.

"Yes, sir," said George. "Whatever you say."

Rider pulled a big key out of a desk drawer and tossed it to George.

"Here," he said. "Go let those boys out of their cells and send them in here to me."

George went to the cells, which were upstairs from the office.

The prisoners were standing by the doors in eager anticipation. George unlocked the cells and pulled open the doors.

"Come on," he said. "The sheriff wants to see you."

The prisoners both knew their way around the jail, so George let them lead the way back into the office. Rider was sitting behind his big desk, his feet propped up on a corner. On the desk in front of him were two handguns besides his own. George recognized the old Remington .44 he had taken from Jesse Halfbreed. The other, an Army Colt .44, he assumed was the one Rider had confiscated from Tom Spike Buck. The two prisoners hesitated just inside the office.

"Come on over here," said Rider.

They walked across the room and stood before the big desk.

"You two remember what you was trying to kill each other for yesterday?" said Rider.

Jesse Halfbreed shifted his weight from one foot to the other, and, keeping his eyes on the floor, he grinned a sheep's grin.

"No, sir, Go-Ahead," he said. "I can't remember nothing. I was too sick."

Tom Spike Buck just looked sullen.

"I don't know," he said.

"You were drunk on whiskey, weren't you?" said Rider.

"Yeah, I guess we were maybe," said Halfbreed, still smiling an ingratiating smile, trying to be friendly. Buck said nothing.

"Where'd you get it?" said Rider.

"Uh, what?" said Halfbreed.

"Where'd you get the whiskey? Who sold it to you?"

"Oh. Well," said Halfbreed, "I can't seem to remember. I—I was pretty sick."

"I don't know," said Buck.

Rider sighed. He picked up Jesse Halfbreed's Remington and dismantled it. Then he did the same with the Colt.

"Put the pieces in your pocket," he said. "You know it's against the law to carry a gun around here. You go home. Both of you. And don't put those back together until you're in your own house."

The two prisoners began picking up the pieces of their pistols and dropping them into pockets. Rider pulled out of his vest pocket the two slips of paper he had gotten from Judge Boley. He handed one slip to each of the men.

"These are your court dates," he said. "You don't show up, either one of you, and I'll come after you, and it'll be worse on you than it is now. Now go on home."

While Tom Spike Buck turned and walked quickly out of the office, Jesse Halfbreed sort of bowed and scraped his way out backward.

"Yes, sir, Go-Ahead," he said. "I'll be there, and I'm going right home now. I'll be there on time. Thank you."

When the two men had left the office, Rider finished off his coffee with one gulp, stood up, and then tucked his two Colts into his waistband.

"*Inena,*" he said.

Even though the last time Rider had said that to him George hadn't responded properly, he did understand the Cherokee command "Let's go," so he followed Rider outside. They went around behind the jail, past the courtyard with the hanging scaffold to a corral and barn which Rider identified as the sheriff's barn. They saddled a couple of horses and rode down the main street. By the capitol building square, Rider stopped and conversed briefly in Cherokee with Beehunter. Then he turned to George.

"Let's go," he said. "Everything's under control here."

They rode to the Capital Hotel, where they dismounted, hitched their horses, and went inside. The proprietor, the same man George had seen the day before, looked up from behind the counter.

"Morning, Sheriff," he said.

"Morning, Bean," said Rider. "This here's my new deputy, George Tanner. George, this is Bean Riley. He owns this place."

"We met yesterday," said George. "Sort of. Good morning, Mr. Riley."

"You found yourself a job right fast, didn't you, Mr. Tanner?" said Riley.

"Well," said George, "the job kind of found me actually, but I'm glad of it."

"What can I do for you?" said Riley.

Rider lounged up against the counter, leaning on one elbow, and he looked sideways at Riley.

"Somebody's been selling whiskey down this way, Bean," he said. "You seen or heard anything that might help me track it down?"

"No. I seen a couple of guys looked like they'd had some, but that's all."

"Who was they?" said Rider.

"Jess Halfbreed and Tom Spike Buck were by here yesterday looking pretty well tanked up."

"That's all?"

"Afraid so, Sheriff."

"Okay," said Rider. "If you hear anything that might help, let us know."

"Sure thing."

Back out at the hitchrail, Rider spoke softly to George.

"Bean is the man we're after," he said. "I know it. The thing is to catch him at it. Get the proof."

The two lawmen moved to their mounts and were about to swing into their saddles when a young woman came walking out of a shop just a couple of doors down the street. She had dark brown hair and brown eyes but fair skin. She was wearing a long pink dress and carrying a parasol. George caught himself staring at her and wishing for a gentlemanly way of making himself known to her. He forced himself to look away, and he began fumbling with the reins of his horse. He watched Rider reach up and touch the brim of his black hat. George made a mental note to add a hat to his want list.

"How do you do, Miss Hunt," said Rider.

"I'm feeling fine, Mr. Rider. Thank you," the lady answered. "It's a lovely morning, isn't it?"

"Yes, ma'am it is. I have someone here I'd like for you to meet,

Miss Hunt. This is my new deputy, George Tanner."

"How do you do, Mr. Tanner," she said.

"Uh, just fine. Thank you, ma'am," George stammered.

"George," said Rider, "this is Miss Lee Hunt. She's taking over the school here next term."

"Oh," said George. "A teacher."

"I'm afraid that remains to be seen, Mr. Tanner. This is my first job."

"I guess that puts us kind of in the same boat," said George. "I'm new at my job, too, and I guess I still have to prove myself."

Rider swung up into the saddle.

"George just finished Harvard," he said. "Classics."

"Oh, really?" said Miss Hunt. "That's wonderful. Perhaps we could get together sometime for a discussion—of the classics."

Rider tipped his hat and turned his horse to move on, so George spoke quickly.

"I'd like that, Miss Hunt," he said. "Right now I guess I have to get back to business. It's certainly been a pleasure meeting you."

Rider was headed north, but George, as he climbed up into the saddle, saw Beehunter running toward them from the opposite direction.

"Rider," he said. "Wait up."

Rider stopped his horse and turned in the saddle.

"What is it?"

George pointed down the street.

"Beehunter," he said.

Rider turned his horse again and rode to meet the running deputy. There was a hurried conversation in Cherokee, then Beehunter turned to go back down to the capitol building. George rode up alongside Rider.

"The chief wants to see us, George," said Rider. "It seems that Mix Hail has disappeared."

Chapter Three

"Rider, Mr. Tanner," Chief Ross was saying, "I can't emphasize strongly enough to you how important the presence of Mix Hail is to this particular council meeting. The vote could swing either way, but without Mix here, the pro-railroaders have got a very good chance of swinging it over to their side."

"Yes, sir," said Rider. "I understand that."

"I hate to have to put it like that," Ross continued. "One man ought to be as important as another in the eyes of the law. It shouldn't matter to you in your capacity as sheriff that Mix is a council member, and it really shouldn't matter which side of any given political issue the man favors. I know all that. Yet the issue is so crucial in my mind that I have to ask you to give it precedence over anything else on your agenda."

"Well, sir," said Rider, "there's really not anything else just now that's too pressing, I guess, and I think we could easily say that a missing council member, especially one as public-minded as old Mix is, calls for some investigation."

"I'm glad you agree," said Ross, standing up and pacing out from behind his massive desk. He walked to the window and stared out over the grounds of the capitol. "Mix wouldn't miss this meeting unless—unless he was severely incapacitated—or . . ."

"Or dead?" Tanner blurted out. He was sorry as soon as he said it, and he thought that he could feel his face redden. "I'm sorry."

"It's all right, George," said Rider. "All you done was to just say what we were all of us thinking."

The chief had gotten back behind his desk by then, and he put his hands down on the desktop and leaned across it toward Rider.

"Rider," he said, "God help me, but I wouldn't put anything past those railroad agents."

"Chief," said Rider, "old Mix is from up in Delaware District. When Council's in session, does he still stop over out at his brother's place?"

"As far as I know, Rider."

"Then that's where we'll start looking."

The chief gave an approving nod, and Rider stood up and put his hat on.

"Come on, George," he said.

Outside the capitol building, Rider stopped on the steps. He stood for a long moment, staring off at nothing in particular.

"George," he said, "you run on back to the office and get us a couple of rifles—just in case. You know where I keep the shells. Get a box of them. Then come on back here."

While Tanner was gone, Rider went back inside. He talked to everyone he could find who might have seen Mix Hail. Then he went back outside to talk to his special deputies. They all told him the same thing. When the Council had broken up the day before,

Mix Hail had left the building and walked toward the livery where he had left his horse and buggy. No one had actually seen him go into the livery or drive out in his buggy. When George Tanner came back with the rifles, Rider and Tanner walked over to where they had left their horses and mounted up.

"Let's ride down to the livery, George," said Rider.

In a few minutes they had their horses hitched in front of the livery, and they went inside the big barn. No one was there. Rider walked over to a buggy standing inside and leaned against it.

"The question's changed, George," he said.

"How's that?"

"I was planning on asking the man what time Mix rode out of here yesterday."

"Yes, sir?" said George.

"This here's old Mix's buggy, and if I ain't mistaken, that's his horse over there."

They walked back out into the street just as a man was running toward the barn. When he saw them he slowed to a fast walk.

"Hey, Rider," he said. "I was just looking for you."

" 'Siyo," said Rider. "Curly, this here's my new deputy, George Tanner. What was you looking for me for?"

"Somebody tried to break into my place last night," said Curly. "Come here. Follow me."

Curly led the way through the barn to a back door and showed the two lawmen where it looked as if someone had tried unsuccessfully to pry it open. The door was barred from the inside. It had no outside latch. The side of the door itself was splintered about two feet along its edge.

"I don't know why they gave it up," said Curly.

"Maybe they heard someone coming along and got scared off," said Rider. "Tell you the truth, I don't know what we can do about it, but we'll kind of keep an eye out. Glad you showed this to us. Curly, we come down here to ask you about Mix Hail."

"What about him?"

"That's his buggy and horse still in there, ain't it?"

"Yeah."

"Did you see him at all yesterday after the meeting was over?"

"Didn't see him before or after. Never seen him at all yesterday."

Rider turned away from Curly, seeming perplexed, then turned back again. Tanner was feeling useless and a little conspicuous.

"Curly," said Rider, "didn't it worry you none when Mix didn't come by here for his rig after the meeting?"

"Why should it?" said Curly. "He told me he'd pick them up when the whole session was done."

"You sure?"

"Sure I'm sure. Hell, it's my business."

"Okay. Thanks, Curly," said Rider. "George, come on."

They climbed on their horses, and Rider led the way around to the side of Curly's barn. There he stopped and dismounted again and squatted down on his haunches. Puzzled, Tanner did the same.

"George," said Rider, "if Curly ain't lying, that means that old Mix was staying in town this time—or somewheres close. He ain't never done that before. He's always stayed over with his brother out by Fourteen Mile Creek. I'm going to ride on out there to see his brother anyhow. While I'm gone, I want you to check around town. I want to know if anyone saw Mix after the meeting, and I want to know where Mix was staying. Go down to the capitol and get Earl Bob to help you. He talks Cherokee, and he knows all the hotels and boardinghouses and such. I'll meet you back at the office later."

Riding west out of Tahlequah toward Fourteen Mile Creek, Rider went over in his mind what he had already learned. Mix Hail, a respected councilman and family man, who in the past had always stayed with his brother while the Council was meeting in Tahlequah, had come to the capital city for the current session and told Curly he would come back for his rig after it was over. Then, the second day of the session, Mix had failed to show. Mix was the primary opponent on the Council of the railroad interests, whose agents were in town applying pressure wherever they could.

There seemed to be two separate puzzles regarding Mix Hail, maybe related, maybe not. Why was Mix not staying at his brother's this time? And why had Mix not attended the second day of the meeting? Well, he thought, the answers are out there—somewhere. I just got to keep looking. But he knew that time was critical. The chief would do what he could to delay discussion of the railroad question in the Council, but the question could not be put off indefinitely. It would be discussed, and it would be voted upon. Rider had to try to find Mix Hail in a hurry. He hoped that Cholly, Mix's brother, would be able to shed some light on the whole situation.

George Tanner walked up to the first of the special deputies he came near. He couldn't remember which one was Earl Bob. He remembered Beehunter, but he knew that he couldn't talk to Beehunter.

"Earl Bob?" he said.

The deputy pointed with his chin toward another man who was standing on the north side and toward the rear of the building.

"*Wado*," said Tanner, feeling a little foolish. The man must know, he thought, that I can't talk Cherokee. He walked toward the other one, the one toward whom he had been directed.

"Earl Bob?"

"Yeah."

"I need your help," said George, feeling some relief. "Rider wants us to go around town and see if we can find out where Mix Hail's been staying. And he wants us to see if we can find anyone who saw Mix Hail yesterday evening after the council meeting."

"Rider said I should go with you?" said Earl Bob.

"Yeah."

"Okay. I better go tell the other guys, though."

Tanner walked with Earl Bob around to the rear of the building to where Beehunter was standing, and Earl Bob spoke to Beehunter in Cherokee. Beehunter made a brief response, and Earl Bob turned back to Tanner.

"Beehunter says he knows where old Mix been staying," he said.

"He does?"

"That's what he says."

"Well," said George, "ask him where."

Again Earl Bob and Beehunter held a brief conversation in Cherokee.

"He said old Mix has got himself a extra girlfriend lately," said Earl Bob. "She lives in Tahlequah, and that's where Mix is staying."

"Find out who she is," said George. "We need to talk to her."

After another brief exchange in Cherokee, Earl Bob looked at the ground and blew some wind out of his mouth.

"Well?" said George.

"Well, I got a name. It's Josie Wicket."

"You know where she lives?"

"Yeah."

"All right," said George. "Let's go."

He had gone four or five steps before he realized that he was walking away alone. He stopped and turned around again to face Earl Bob.

"Come on," he said. "What's wrong?"

"Beehunter says that Josie won't talk to you and me. She won't tell us nothing."

Tanner reached up to scratch his head, and he wished that he had a hat on that he would have had to shove it back on his head in order to do that.

"Well," he said, "what do we do then? Will she talk to him?"

"He thinks so."

"Tell him to go see her. Talk to her. Find out what he can about where Mix Hail has been, what he's been doing. Mainly we want to know if that's where he's been staying, and we want to know where he went after yesterday's meeting. When did she see him last? Tell him all that, and then tell him to get right back down here."

Beehunter took off, and George wondered what he should do next. If he took Earl Bob and started making the rounds of the hotels and boardinghouses the way Rider had told him to do, there would only be three special deputies left at the capitol. Rider had hired five men to guard the building. Taking one away might be all right, but George didn't feel as if he had the authority to cut the force down to three. He could go by himself, but he probably wouldn't get much accomplished. After all, Rider had told him to take Earl Bob along. Rider obviously didn't think that George could find out much by himself. Maybe he and Earl Bob should just wait there at the capitol for Beehunter to get back and then go out. All at once, George felt foolish. He was glad that he had kept his thoughts to himself. The reason he was supposed to go out with Earl Bob was to find out where Mix Hail had been staying. They had already found that out.

"Earl Bob," he said, "you stay here. I'll be back later to see what Beehunter found out."

As Rider pulled up in front of Cholly Hail's house on Fourteen Mile Creek, the front door of the house opened and Cholly stepped out.

" *'Siyo*, Go-Ahead," he said.

" *'Siyo*, Cholly. How's things going with you?"

"Not too bad. Come on in the house and have a cup of coffee."

Rider swung down out of the saddle and hitched his horse to the rail fence.

"Your missus inside?" he asked.

"Yeah."

"I need to talk to you alone," said Rider.

"Well, all right."

"I just found out, Cholly, that Mix ain't been staying out here with you. He's always stayed with you during council sessions before this, ain't he?"

"Yeah," said Cholly. "Up till now."

"Anything wrong between you two?"

"No. Not that I know of. Mix came by when he got in. He ate with us. Then he said that he'd be staying in town this trip. That's all he said."

"He didn't say where he'd be staying or who he'd be staying with?"

"No, he didn't."

Rider took off his hat and wiped the sweat off his brow with a shirtsleeve. He leaned on the top rail of the fence and looked off toward the creek.

"Cholly, have you see Mix since then?" he asked.

"No, I ain't. Go-Ahead, what's wrong? Has something happened to Mix? I got a right to know. He's my brother."

"Hell, I know that, Cholly," said Rider. "That's why I'm here. I don't know. Mix didn't show up this morning. I'm trying to find him. Trying to find out why he didn't show. That's all so far."

Tanner left his horse at the capitol and started walking down Muskogee Avenue. He hesitated in front of Bean Riley's Capital Hotel, then went inside.

"Tanner," said Riley, "back so soon?"

"I'm doing a little investigating," said Tanner. "Last night, after the council meeting, did you see Mix Hail anywhere?"

"Can't say I did," said Riley.

"Well, thanks," said Tanner. He stepped back outside, again feeling useless and foolish. Was this police work? Would Rider have done anything differently? What would Rider do next if he were here right now? He resumed his walk down the street, but he didn't go inside any more places. He didn't question any more citizens. He wondered if he had done the right thing when he had accepted Rider's offer of a job. He certainly didn't feel as if he was earning money. He just didn't know what to do.

Chapter Four

Rider was just a few miles outside of Tahlequah when he turned his horse off onto a rocky trail going south. It was barely wide enough for a wagon to pass through, and it was canopied over by the branches of tall oak and walnut trees. The woods were thick with a heavy undergrowth of brush and brambles that extended to the sides of the road. The trees came alive with the scolding chatter of gray squirrels and the songs of cardinals, blue jays, and mockingbirds. Now and then the insistent, overbearing *ga ga* of a distant crow sounded above the other noises. He rode a couple of miles down this road and stopped in front of a small log cabin. Beside the cabin was a brush arbor. In this arbor an old man sat.

"Come in," said the old man, speaking in Cherokee. "I've been waiting for you here."

Rider dismounted and hitched his horse to a small cottonwood beside the road. Close to the cottonwood was a large tree stump. Rider pulled the Colts out of his waistband and laid them on the stump. Then he walked into the arbor.

" *'Siyo,* White Tobacco," he said. "I need your help."

"Sit down."

The arbor was hung around on all sides with a variety of plants in various stages of drying, and on the ground under the roof were baskets, jugs, crocks, and boxes filled with tobacco, herbs, and other curiosities stashed in disarray. There was a small table in the center and on each side of the table, a chair. White Tobacco sat in one chair, smoking a corncob pipe. Rider sat in the other chair.

"What's your trouble?" said White Tobacco.

"A man is missing," said Rider. "I have to find him."

White Tobacco puffed on his pipe for a long while. Clouds of blue-gray smoke hovered around his head, half concealing his grizzled old visage from Rider's view. Finally he spoke again.

"You're the sheriff," he said. "You get paid for these things."

"Yes," said Rider. "I know, but this one is very important to the Cherokee Nation. There's an urgency to the situation. The Council is meeting, and the missing man is a councilman. If we don't find him soon and get him back to the meeting, the others may vote for the railroad to come into Tahlequah."

Again White Tobacco sat and puffed and thought.

"What is the man's name?" he asked.

"The missing man is Mix Hail."

"Wait," said White Tobacco, and he got up from his chair and moved slowly and methodically around the small space in the arbor, rummaging through baskets and boxes. Finally he went back to his chair and sat down. From his wrinkled, leathery old hands, he poured onto the table some colored beads, a crystal, and a lump of red ocher tied to a length of string.

"Now," he said, "we'll see what we can see."

After he had walked the length of Muskogee Avenue and back again, George rejoined Earl Bob on the capitol grounds. Beehunter had not yet returned. He decided that he could be just as useless and not nearly so conspicuous in the office. He told Earl Bob where he would be, took his horse back to the sheriff's barn, and went into the office. The fire in the stove was nearly out, so he built that up enough to boil water, and he made some coffee. He tried to make it just the way he had seen Rider do it. Then he settled down at his desk to wait. After he had gone through about half of his fresh pot of coffee, which, he immediately decided, was not nearly as good as the one Rider had made earlier, Earl Bob came into the office. George stood up, he thought, a little too quickly, too anxiously.

"Is Beehunter back?" he asked.

"Yeah. Josie said, yeah, old Mix has been staying with her, but she was worried, she said, 'cause he didn't come by last night. She fed him breakfast yesterday morning, then she never seen him again. She's worried."

"You know where she lives, right?" asked George.

"Yeah, but like I said before, she won't talk to us."

"I don't want to talk to her," said George. "I want you to walk me to her house—from the capitol."

Earl Bob shrugged, and the two deputies left the office and walked to the capitol, where Earl Bob said something to Beehunter in Cherokee. George thought they were probably talking about him.

"Let's go," said George.

Earl Bob started walking north, parallel to but east of Muskogee Avenue. George's first thought was that if people had seen Mix Hail leave the capitol and walk toward the livery, which was south from the capitol on Muskogee, then Mix could not have been going directly to Josie Wicket's house. He had to have gone somewhere else. Still, George let Earl Bob lead him all the way to the woman's house. It was on the northwest edge of town—really just outside of town. George could see how Mix Hail might have been able to spend some time discreetly at this place. It was off the road, accessible only by a footpath through thick woods, and only a small area was cleared around it for a yard. It was not likely that anyone would just happen by. Anyone coming to Josie Wicket's house would have to be either lost or a deliberate visitor. George wondered how Beehunter had known that Mix Hail was staying there.

"Be a good place to waylay someone," he said.

It was not long after George had left Earl Bob back at the capitol and gone back to the office that Rider returned. He walked in and went straight to the coffeepot on the stove. George was glad that he had made some fresh coffee, but he wondered if Rider would notice that it was not as good as his. Rider poured himself a cup and went to his desk.

"What did you find out, *chooj*?" he said.

"Well," said George, "Mix Hail had been staying with a woman named Josie Wicket."

Rider put down his cup and looked directly at George, his face registering surprise.

"You sure about that?" he asked.

"Beehunter knew, but I sent him up to question her anyway. Earl Bob said that she wouldn't talk to us. According to Beehunter, she confirmed it. She also said that he had breakfast with her yesterday morning, and she hasn't seen him since then. She's worried about him, so she must have expected him to come back last night. Course this is all secondhand with me. It was Earl Bob who told me what Beehunter said."

"Yeah," said Rider. "Okay. So old Mix was shacked up with Josie Wicket. I'll be. I wonder how I missed out on that bit of news."

"I didn't ask," said George, "but I wonder how Beehunter knew."

"Josie's his sister-in-law," said Rider, "his wife's sister."

"Oh," said George. He still didn't understand why Beehunter would automatically know about a clandestine affair between his wife's sister and a respected councilman, but the explanation obviously was sufficient for Rider. He let it go.

"Anything else?" asked Rider.

"I had Earl Bob walk me to Josie Wicket's house. I didn't see anything along the way, but two thoughts came to my mind. One was that the trail to that house would be a likely spot for an ambush. But the other is that the people who saw Mix Hail leave the capitol yesterday said he was headed toward the livery. He wasn't going in the direction of Josie Wicket's house."

"Good thinking, George. You're going to do all right here."

George stood up and walked to the stove with his cup. He poured himself some more coffee, then turned to face Rider.

"I spent a lot of time today doing nothing," he said. "I walked down the street and back, and I sat in here waiting for Beehunter to get back and after that just waiting for you. I didn't know what else to do."

Rider smiled.

"George," he said, "you just learned something about police work. Lots of times you just sit and wait. You'll learn to live with it, not worry about it. You done good today. You found out more than I did."

"What did you find out?" asked George.

"Just that old Mix stopped by Cholly's house—that's his brother—when he first got here, ate a meal with them, and told them that he was going to be staying in town this trip. They ain't seen him since then."

"So what do we do from here?"

"Somebody had to see old Mix go somewhere," said Rider. "He left the capitol walking toward the livery, but he didn't go to the livery. Come on, let's take a walk."

Rider, with George following along, walked over to the capitol and started from there toward the livery barn where Mix Hail's horse and buggy were stashed. He stopped at every business along the way, asking the same question: "Did you see Mix Hail walk past here last evening?"

Some of the businessmen said they had been too busy at the time to have noticed anything, but several did say that they had seen him pass by. The last one to give that positive response was Alfred Kirk of Al's Eats, just about halfway down toward the livery.

"Sure," said Kirk. "I was getting ready for my busy time, you know, dinner hour. So I was kind of watching out in the street to see who might come in. That's how come me to remember. Mix walked up like he was in kind of a hurry, but then he stopped. Right out there. I thought sure he was coming in, but then he walked on."

"Did you see where he went?" asked Rider.

"Naw, he passed on by my window there, and that's all I seen of him."

Al Kirk had been the last of the Muskogee Avenue merchants to have seen Mix Hail.

"Well," said Rider to George, standing back out on the sidewalk, "we know he got this far, but we still don't know where he was going. He either turned east or west off of Muskogee, or somebody stopped him, or someone's lying to us. Now we got to figure out which one."

"If anyone had stopped him here against his will," said George, "that is, by use of force, someone would have seen it. It was still broad daylight."

"Yeah. You're right. Listen, George, Exie's going to have our dinner on the table here in a minute, and all these folks along here will be closing up to go home, too. You go on up to the house and tell Exie for me that I'll be along directly. I need to stop by and see the chief. I know he's worried about this Mix Hail case."

Later that evening, following their meal, Rider and Tanner were again out in the dog run with coffee. Rider was smoking his pipe.

"George," said Rider, "first thing in the morning we got to approach this thing from another direction. I'm going to pull all but two of the boys off of the capitol detail. We're going to question everyone between the capitol and Al's place, and then east and west from Al's. We're going to ask them to recall everything they saw last evening. Who was out on the street? Did they see anything unusual? Like that, see. We find out who else was out there on the street, then we track them down and ask them the same questions.

Somewhere along the line someone's going to tell us where Mix went to. I'm putting you in charge of that. I'll tell the boys in the morning."

"Yes, sir," said George.

Rider took a sip from his coffee cup, set it aside, and puffed contemplatively on his pipe for a long, silent moment. Somewhere in the night a whippoorwill sounded its lonesome call.

"While you're doing that," said Rider, "I'm going to start to harass those railroad fellows."

The evening was still young when Rider had finished his pipe and was thinking about having another cup of coffee, when Delbert Swim came walking up to the dog run, a little winded from having just walked up the hill to Rider's house.

"'*Siyo,* Del," said Rider.

"Go-Ahead," said Swim, speaking Cherokee, "you better come down."

"What is it?" said Rider.

Swim then noticed Tanner seated across the dog run from Rider, and he decided to switch to English in deference to the new deputy.

"They just brought in Mix Hail," he said. "He's dead."

Chapter Five

"Don't seem as if he's been dead long," said Rider. "Judging by the shape the body's in. Plus he was found out on the road to Fourteen Mile Creek, and I just traveled that road not four hours ago. One gunshot wound to the heart. Close range, too. I'd say the gun was stuck up against his chest and fired. No money in his pockets."

Delbert Swim handed a Remington .44 six-shooter to Rider.

"This was found beside him, Rider," he said. "One shot's been fired."

Rider took the pistol, but he gave it only a cursory glance.

"Okay, Delbert," he said. "Where's the folks that found him?"

"They're over at your office, waiting for you."

"George," said Rider, "go over there and take down their statements, will you? Get as much detail out of them as you can. And get them to sign the statements. Delbert will go with you. I've got to go tell Chief Ross."

Rider left the body there in the undertaker's parlor and went to the sheriff's barn for his horse. Then he rode to Park Hill to see Chief Ross. It was late when he returned to Tahlequah, but George Tanner was still in the office, with the lamp burning. Rider read the statements that George had taken. There wasn't much information. Rider knew the people who had discovered the body, two full-blood Cherokees, a husband and wife. They had been on their way home from Tahlequah when they came across the remains of Mix Hail in the middle of the road just about five miles out of town. The body had been lying facedown, the Remington right at its head.

Rider decided to visit the site in the morning, though he didn't expect to find anything there.

"You want some coffee, Rider?" said George.

"Yeah," said Rider with a sigh.

George poured a cup of the coffee he had brewed while waiting for Rider to return from Park Hill. He placed the cup on Rider's desk, then went back to his own chair.

"Wado, chooj," said Rider. He picked up the cup and sipped some coffee. "George, something's wrong here."

"If Mix Hail was just killed in the last four hours," said George, "where was he between the time Alfred Kirk saw him yesterday evening and the time he was killed?"

Rider nodded his head slowly in agreement.

"That's part of it," he said.

"There's somewhere between twenty and twenty-four hours unaccounted for."

"Yeah. And there's more. How did he get out there on that road? His horse and buggy are in town. He was on foot. Did someone kill him somewhere else and then carry him out there? I think so. There was straw stuck to his clothes and in the hair on the back of his head—like he'd been laying on his back in it. He was found facedown on a dirt road."

He took another sip of coffee.

"And then there's this," he said. He picked up the Remington and held it up for George to see. "You ever see this before?"

George got up and walked over to Rider's desk, where he squinted at the gun.

"It's a Remington .44," he said, "like Jesse Halfbreed's. Is it Jesse's?"

"It is," said Rider. "But if Jesse killed Mix, which I don't believe, why would he leave his gun there for us to find?"

"Panic, maybe," said George, "or maybe he was drunk again."

"A drunk man might kill someone and drop his gun, but I don't think he'd haul the body off somewhere and drop the gun there. It don't make sense to me."

"I see what you mean."

"I know Jess," Rider continued. "This ain't like him. When he gets drunk and does something stupid, he does it right out in the open. You saw that."

"Yeah," said George. He went back to his own desk and sat down. He thought for a moment in silence. "You think whoever killed Mix Hail put that gun there so we'd think Jesse Halfbreed was the killer?"

"I think that's a strong possibility," said Rider. "Course there's others. Jess could have sold the gun or traded it for whiskey. Anything's possible. We'll ask him in the morning."

By morning Rider had reordered his priorities. He sent three deputies out to question the people in the area previously defined as being where Mix Hail had last been seen alive, leaving Beehunter and Earl Bob at the capitol, and he took Tanner with him to examine the site on the road where the body had been discovered. There were two other important jobs to be done, and Rider considered sending George off alone to see to at least one of them, but he had decided against that. He told himself that now that they were in fact investigating a murder, there was no virtue in taking chances. No one should go out alone. He wondered, though, if he simply didn't trust George yet with anything really important. Well, he thought, whatever the reason, the decision's been made.

They located the spot easily based on landmarks the Cherokee couple had described, and Rider was totally satisfied when he found a trace of blood and some bits of straw in the middle of the road.

"See this, George," he said. "This straw got here off the body. There's no straw around here. Just this. Right where somebody dumped poor old Mix."

"So it seems," said George. "He was killed somewhere else."

They looked around for a few more minutes, finding nothing, and then Rider climbed back into his saddle.

"Let's go see Jess Halfbreed," he said.

"What about all these tracks?" said George.

"That's just the problem, George. There's too many of them to do us any good. Come on."

No one was home at Jesse Halfbreed's house. Rider told George to look around the outside of the house while he checked the inside. He noticed right away that there were no women's clothes in the house. He could find nothing else of any use or interest, so he went outside to find George.

"Looks like Jesse's woman packed up and left him," he said. "You see anything?"

George pointed off toward the woods behind the house.

"About halfway to the trees," he said. "Looks like a jug."

Rider walked out toward the object, George following. It was a jug. Rider picked it up and sniffed at its mouth.

"Whiskey," he said. "It's empty. What's that?"

He was pointing to another object in the grass, halfway again to the trees. This time George trotted ahead to check. Rider walked behind him.

"It's a shoe," said George.

Rider looked from the shoe to the woods, then back toward the cabin.

"George," he said, "I got a suspicious thought in my head

that tells me that somebody's trying to lead us to something."

He started walking toward the woods, following a straight line drawn from the house through the jug and the shoe. George felt the handle of the Starr revolver hanging at his side for reassurance, then he started to follow Rider. George was looking down as he entered the woods to make sure he didn't trip over a fallen branch or stumble on uneven ground. He hadn't taken more than six steps when he came up abruptly on Rider, standing still. He looked up. Jesse Halfbreed was hanging from a branch of a red oak tree.

"Oh, my God," said George.

Jesse Halfbreed's hands were not tied. There was a nail keg lying on its side just a few feet away, and right at the base of the tree from which the body dangled, one shoe off, was a pile of paper money and loose change, the bills held down by an egg-sized rock. After Rider had counted the money, which came to $47.23, and replaced the rock, he sat down wearily on the ground and leaned back against a tree. George was still staring at the body. It was swinging only slightly and turning slowly, but the movement was enough to cause the rope to creak noisily as it rubbed against the branch.

"What's it look like, George?" said Rider.

George didn't answer immediately, and Rider couldn't tell whether it was because he was about to be sick or because he was trying to formulate a response.

"Looks like suicide," said George. "Looks like he climbed up on that keg and put the noose around his own neck and then kicked over the keg."

Rider gestured toward the cash at the base of the tree.

"What about that?" he said.

"Some kind of a message. Like a suicide note almost. I'd say we're supposed to read it that he took that money off Mix Hail's body and then got remorseful over the whole thing."

"Yeah," said Rider. "What else?"

"Well, the jug and the shoe were pointers, a kind of a trail that began with the Remington left by Mix Hail's body."

Rider waited. George took a deep breath and then stepped up close to the body. He walked around it, looking closely.

"No straw," he said. "Jesse Halfbreed did not move Mix Hail's body, and that probably means that he didn't kill him either. This whole thing's a setup."

Rider got himself back on his feet and reached into a pocket for his penknife.

"Let's cut him down, George," he said. "We got a lot of work to do."

Rider and Tanner found Omer Lyons in the lobby of the Capital Hotel, and Rider walked straight to where Lyons was sitting in one of the overstuffed lounge chairs, reading the latest copy of *The Cherokee Advocate,* probably, Rider thought, trying to figure out how Cherokee public opinion was going on the railroad issue. When the two lawmen walked in, Riley sidled back behind his counter and hunkered there.

"Hello, Lyons," said Rider.

Lyons looked up from behind his paper.

"This here's my deputy, George Tanner."

Lyons shot a sidelong glance toward Tanner. He still didn't speak.

"I'll get right to it, Lyons," said Rider. "I guess you've heard that Mix Hail has been murdered."

"That's too bad," said Lyons.

"It's not too bad for your purposes, though, is it?"

Lyons put down his newspaper and stood up, immediately defensive. He was a man probably not yet forty, tall and straight with a receding hairline, dressed in an expensive, though conservative, gray business suit. Tanner thought, this man's a citizen? By marriage or by blood? If by blood, he couldn't be more than one-thirty-second Indian.

"No," said Lyons, "it's not. Just good luck, I guess. I hope you're not implying anything further by that observation."

"I'm just investigating a murder, Mr. Lyons," said Rider. "So far you're the only person I know of, you and your railroad associates, who had anything to gain from Mix Hail's death. I ain't accusing you of anything—yet. Just making a—what did you call it?—a observation. By the way, can you account for your whereabouts yesterday evening from about, say, four o'clock?"

"Yes, I can," said Lyons, "and I will if I have to."

"You might," said Rider. "We'll be watching you." He turned to leave the hotel, George following close behind. Out in the street, George hurried up beside Rider.

"What was that all about?" he said.

"I just want him nervous," said Rider. "That's all."

"You think he did it?"

"I don't know, George. Like I said, he's the only one I know of just now with a reason for it."

"What about Mix Hail's—lady?" said George.

"That would give his wife a motive, if she knew about it. We don't know that she did."

Rider sent George to round up the three deputies he had detailed that morning on special assignment and told him to bring them to the office for a special meeting. He would be there soon, he said. He stopped on his way to report to Chief Ross, and he found the chief still worried about the vote on the railroad issue.

"I can't put it off after today, Rider," the chief said. "The Council will bring it to a vote tomorrow, I'm sure, and I'm afraid of the outcome."

From the chief's office, Rider went to find Deputy U.S. Marshal Elwood Lovely.

"Unless we know there's a white man involved, I can't touch it," said Lovely. "You know that. But I am curious, and with your permission, I'd like to sit in on your little meeting."

"Come on," said Rider.

At Rider's office they found George and the three special deputies waiting. George had the coffee made, and he poured it all the way around. Everyone found himself a chair, Rider pulling his two Colts out of his waistband before sitting down behind his desk. He laid the Colts on the desktop in front of him, then he introduced

George Tanner to Elwood Lovely. The special deputies already knew the deputy marshal.

"Here's what we've got," he said. "Day before yesterday the Council meeting broke up around four-thirty. Mix Hail was seen walking from the capitol building toward the livery barn. The last person to see him on Muskogee Avenue, so far as we know, was Al Kirk. He never made it to the livery, if that's where he was headed. The next morning, yesterday morning, he never showed up for the meeting. He was reported to us as missing. We found out that he'd been staying in Tahlequah at the home of Josie Wicket. Last night some folks found his body out on the road to Fourteen Mile Creek. He'd been shot once in the chest at close range. There was no money on him, and there was pieces of straw stuck to his clothes and his hair. No straw anywhere near where the body was found. We think he was killed somewhere else and moved out there. Jesse Halfbreed's old Remington six-shooter was found in the road by the body. It had been fired.

"Me and George went to see Jesse, and we found him hanging from a tree limb out in the woods behind his house. It seemed like there was a kind of trail leading us to him from the house, a jug and a shoe. There was cash money at the foot of the tree. That's it. Unless you boys found out anything today."

"We've already talked that out while we were waiting for you, Rider," said George. "There's nothing new. Nobody else seems to have seen Mix Hail. The boys checked every house and every place of business along the way—uh, except for one."

"What one?"

"Miss Hunt lives on the side street there going east. She wasn't home."

Rider stood up, picked up his coffee cup, and walked to the stove to refill the cup. He turned back toward the others in the room and took a sip from the hot coffee.

"She's probably home by now," he said. "Why don't you run on over there and have a talk with her?"

George looked self-consciously around the room. No one seemed to be responding to Rider's suggestion. He pointed foolishly at his own chest with a thumb.

"Me?" he said.

"She's a schoolteacher. You're a Harvard man. You're the only one around here with enough education to talk to her. Go on."

George stood for a moment, looking stupid, he thought, and awaiting further discussion. No one said anything. He looked at the floor, then he glanced back up at Rider.

"You mean now?" he said.

"You got any reason to put it off?" asked Rider.

"Well, uh, no, sir," said George. "Well, I guess I'll just take a run over there and ask her some questions. I shouldn't be long."

"Take your time, George," said Rider. "We'll probably break up here in a minute or two anyhow. We can talk later about what you find out."

Chapter Six

George thought about saddling a horse from the sheriff's barn to ride over to Lee Hunt's house, but he decided not to bother. He walked. It wasn't far, and besides that, he wanted the time to think about how he would approach her. He was being silly, he knew. He was on official business. He was not going on a social call. He knew what questions needed to be asked, so there was really no reason to worry about what he would say, how he would present himself to Miss Hunt. He would present himself as Go-Ahead Rider's deputy, explain the purpose of the visit, and ask the questions that needed to be answered. Then he would thank her for her cooperation and take his leave.

But would that make him seem to her to be cold and indifferent? He certainly did not want to leave her with that impression. He wanted badly to get better acquainted with her. He wanted an excuse to call on her, and Rider had given him one. Must he be all business on this occasion?

He had not managed to resolve these questions by the time he had reached her house, and he stepped up to her door nervously. He lifted his fist, hesitated, then knocked. He shifted his weight from one foot to the other. He turned his head and looked off down the street in the direction from which he had come, then looked back at the door. He raised his hand to knock again, and while it hovered there almost beside his head, the door was opened. Miss Hunt's expression betrayed pleasant surprise.

"Why, Mr. Tanner," she said.

"I'm sorry to just drop in on you like this unannounced," said George. "It's, uh, it's official business."

"It's perfectly all right, Mr. Tanner. Please come in."

Lee Hunt stepped aside to allow George room to walk through the doorway. After he was inside, she shut the door behind him and motioned to a chair.

"Please sit down," she said.

George moved to the chair a bit awkwardly, then sat.

"Thank you," he said.

"Would you like a cup of tea?"

"Oh, no, thank you. Don't go to any trouble. I won't take much of your time."

"I just made myself a pot of tea," she said. "It's no trouble at all."

"Well, then, yes. Thank you."

Lee Hunt moved to get the teacups and fill them. As she brought George a cup, she spoke again.

"What possible official business could the sheriff's office have with me?"

"We're trying to trace the movements of Mix Hail when he was last seen," said George. "The day he disappeared, he was seen down on the avenue, but not beyond where it intersects with your street. As far as we've been able to determine, no one except his killer saw him after that. We've talked to all your neighbors, and none of them saw him either. You're the last one on this street. I have to ask you if you saw Mr. Hail out here on the street at any time that day."

"What day was that, Mr. Tanner? I don't know—I mean, I didn't know Mr. Hail. I knew his name, of course. He was a councilman, but as far as I know, I never saw him."

"Well, it, uh, it would have been the day before yesterday, Miss Hunt, in the late afternoon or early evening."

"I did see something out there that was unusual that day. I don't know if it was Mr. Hail or not. I heard the sound of a horse and buggy out in the street, and I looked out the window. The buggy stopped just down the hill, almost in front of the next house, my neighbors', the Thompsons' house. Mr. Riley stepped out of the buggy and walked back down toward Muskogee Avenue. I suppose it was none of my business, but I kept watching, because it seemed curious to me that he would drive up here, then walk back down the hill. The Thompsons were not at home. I already knew that."

"You said Mr. Riley. Would that be—"

"Bean, I believe is his first name. Mr. Bean Riley. The owner of the Capital Hotel."

"Thank you," said George. "Did you see him come back to the buggy?"

"He came back in a few minutes with another man. They seemed to be in a heated discussion over something. I couldn't hear anything they said. Then they both got into the buggy and drove off."

"Which direction did they go?"

"West."

"So they didn't go back down to the avenue."

"No."

George tipped up his teacup and emptied it.

"Would you like some more?" asked Lee.

"Well, uh, yes, please."

Lee stood up and got the teapot. She refilled George's cup, then her own, put the teapot back on the table, then sat back down.

"Can you describe the man who got into the buggy with Mr. Riley?" said George.

"Not very well, I'm afraid," said Lee. "He was, I would say, middle-aged. He was well dressed, wearing a suit. I think it was a black suit. He was a bit portly, I'd say. Not fat. Portly. He had a beard. Not long, but full. And—he was wearing a hat."

"What kind of a hat?"

"Well, it was a wide-brimmed hat. No, not really wide. Medium, I guess, and flat, and it had a short, round crown. It was light colored. Not white. Tan or beige, I guess. I'm sorry I can't be more specific, but, of course, I had no idea that I'd ever be asked to describe the man, and I did feel just a bit nosy for even watching as much as I did."

"I'm glad you did, Miss Hunt," said George, "and I think that your description was very good. In fact, I think you've just described Mix Hail. The only thing is, I've not seen the hat."

George was suddenly nervous again. He realized all at once that he had no more official questions for Lee Hunt, and that meant that his excuse for remaining in her company was gone. He had a little more tea in his cup. He looked down at it, then he lifted the cup and drank the tea. He stood nervously and looked for a place to put the cup. Lee stood up and took it from him.

"Well," he said, "I guess that's it. Thank you very much. You've been a big help, I think. I, uh, I guess I'd better be going."

He stepped to the door, and as he grasped the handle to open it, Lee spoke again.

"Mr. Tanner?"

He turned his head too quickly to face her, too anxiously, he thought.

"Yes?"

"Please come back when you have more time—just for a visit."

Her face turned just a bit red, and George could see that she had embarrassed herself by being too forward. He was ashamed of himself. He should have made that move, not forced her to do it. He felt his own face flush, and he looked down at the floor.

"I'd like that," he said. "I'd like that very much. Thank you."

"Good night, Mr. Tanner."

"Good night, Miss Hunt."

Outside George took deep breaths of fresh night air, and he walked back to the office in long, quick strides. He felt a tremendous sense of relief. In her house he had felt nervous, anxious, ill at ease. Outside he felt as if he had been released from a cage. Yet he was sorry to have left her company. The next visit, he told himself, would be better. The next time he would know that he was welcome. She had actually asked him to return. He would handle himself better the next time. He would be more relaxed.

He was back at the office almost before he knew it, and he found it dark. Rider had said that they would be gone before he got back. He tried the door anyway, and it was locked. He started walking toward Rider's house.

Rider was sitting alone in the dog run smoking his pipe when George came up to the house. It was dark already, and Rider heard the footsteps before he could see the form that came with them.

"That you, George?"

"Yeah."

George moved on into the dog run and found the other chair. He sat down.

"Kids in bed already?" he asked.

"Yeah. I'm just having another smoke before I turn in. Coffee's still hot. You want some?"

"Yeah," said George. "Thanks. I can get it."

"No. You just set there."

Rider went into the house and soon reemerged with two cups of coffee. He handed one to George and sat back down.

"How was your visit?" he said.

"What?"

"You did go see Miss Hunt, didn't you?"

"Oh," said George. "Yeah. It was real nice. She's, uh, she's a real nice lady, Miss Hunt. She has a nice little house over there. Real nice. She gave me some tea."

Rider puffed his pipe, then removed it from his mouth and took a sip of hot coffee.

"That sounds nice," he said.

"Yeah," said George. "It was. It was real nice. She invited me back, too."

"Good," said Rider. "I'm glad to hear that your social life is picking up."

"Yeah," said George, and he gave a short, nervous laugh. "I guess it is. I, uh, I guess I ought to thank you for sending me over there tonight. I might not ever have gotten around to it on my own. I'm glad you sent me. Thanks, Rider."

"Yeah, I did send you over there, didn't I?"

"Yeah."

"George?"

"Yeah?"

Rider puffed at his pipe, but the fire had gone out. He tapped it on the side of his chair to knock out the dead ashes.

"George," he said, "what did I send you over there for?"

"Oh," said George, suddenly glad of the darkness, for he felt his face flush hot. "Oh, yeah. Well. She saw him, Rider. I mean, she said she never knew Mix Hail, but from her description, I feel pretty sure that she saw him. Bean Riley drove a buggy up there and stopped it just below her house. In front of her neighbor's place. Then Bean walked back down to Muskogee Avenue, and pretty soon he came back up to the buggy with another man. She described the other man, and I think it was Mix Hail. Both men got into the buggy and drove off west."

"Bean Riley, huh?"

"Yes, sir. Bean Riley."

"I'll bet," said Rider, "that Lyons has got ole Bean on the railroad lobby's payroll."

"You seem pretty sure that the railroad's behind all this," said George.

"It's the only thing that makes any sense, George. The only thing."

"Rider?"

"Yeah?"

"This might not be important. I don't know. But Mix Hail—if that's who Miss Hunt saw get into the buggy—Mix Hail was wearing a hat. We never found a hat."

"She describe the hat to you?"

"Light colored. Tan or beige, she said. Medium width, flat brim, and a low, round crown."

"That's Mix's hat. Sounds like."

George took a sip of his coffee. It was still hot, almost too hot to drink. He put the cup down on the table, stood up, and paced away from Rider, toward the street. He rested his right hand on the butt of the Starr revolver hanging at his side and stared off into the darkness beyond.

"So what do we do now?" he asked. "We going to arrest Mr. Riley?"

"What's the charge, George?" asked Rider.

"Well, suspicion of murder, I guess."

Rider finished his coffee and put the cup down. Then he pulled a tobacco pouch out of his vest pocket and started to refill his pipe.

"I do suspicion him," he said, "but that's all we got. We can't arrest him for driving ole Mix somewhere in his buggy."

George walked back to his chair and sat down.

"What then?" he said.

Rider struck a match, and the flame burst out in the darkness. He lit his pipe and took several puffs to make sure it was going well.

"I think we'll just let it rest awhile, George," he said. "Go back to the whiskey case. Work on that."

"What?"

"Sleep on it. Think about it. We'll talk about it some more in the morning."

George tossed in his bed that night. Why would Rider abandon a murder case—one that Chief Ross was particularly concerned about—to chase down a whiskey seller? That didn't make any sense. If it had been anyone besides Rider, George would have thought him a fool or an incompetent, but he couldn't think either of those things about Go-Ahead Rider. No. Rider knew what he was doing. But George didn't know, and that frustrated George. The selling of illegal whiskey was a serious crime; George knew that. And in the absence of a murder, it would make perfect sense to concentrate on that problem. But George couldn't help but think that the murder should take precedence. What was Rider thinking? "Go back to the whiskey case," he had said. That had been Rider's top priority before the disappearance of Mix Hail. George had accompanied Rider on his visit to the Capital Hotel when Rider questioned Riley about that, and—wait a minute, thought George. What had Rider said? "Bean is the man we're after." He'd said that just after they had left the hotel. Bean Riley was the whiskey seller. At least that's what Rider believed. And now they knew that Bean Riley was the last man seen with Mix Hail. It began to make sense.

George was awake early the next morning. He hadn't slept much the night before, but he wasn't sleepy, and he wasn't tired. He was wide awake and anxious to start the day.

He looked across the dog run to the other cabin and saw no evidence that anyone was up yet over there. He dressed, strapped on the Starr revolver, and went out to sit in the dog run. In less than a minute he was up and pacing out to the road. He pulled the Illinois Railroad watch out of his vest pocket and checked the time. Damn, he said to himself. He was up too early. It would be an hour before breakfast, at least a half hour before Rider would stir. He paced back to the chair, but he knew that he wouldn't be able to stand the wait. He took a little notebook and a pencil out of his pocket, and he penciled a note to Rider.

Going downtown for breakfast. See you at the office.

George

He put the note on the table in the dog run, knowing that Rider would be out there with his first cup of coffee and weighed it down with a small rock, then he began walking down the hill. He walked past the jail and on down to Muskogee Avenue as far as Al's Eats. He went inside, sat down, and when Al came over to his table, ordered himself a big breakfast of eggs, sausage, biscuits, and gravy. He drank three cups of coffee while he was waiting for the breakfast, another with the meal, and two more after he had finished eating.

He pulled the watch out of his pocket and checked the time. In another fifteen minutes, Rider would be at the office. He thought about having one more cup of coffee to pass the time, but his stomach was already sloshing from the previous six cups. He decided against it, got up, paid for his breakfast, and turned to walk out the door. Just then the door opened, and Omer Lyons and Bean Riley walked in together. George gave them a nod as he left. Outside he hesitated. He looked back through the window and saw them sit down together. He wanted to be sure. Yes. They sat down together. He walked on to the office.

The office was still locked up when George got there, so he started walking back up the hill, back toward Rider's house. About halfway up the hill, he saw Rider coming down. He hurried to meet him.

"You got out early this morning, George," said Rider.

"Yeah," said George, turning to walk alongside Rider. "I've been thinking. I know what you're up to. At least I think I do."

"All right," said Rider. "Tell me about it."

"You think that Bean Riley is the man who's been selling whiskey around here. Right?"

"Right."

"But you also think that Bean is guilty of Mix Hail's murder—or at the least, he's involved in it. Right?"

"Right again."

"Well, we've got nothing to go on with the murder case. I mean, we've got a lot of evidence, but nothing that really points to anyone.

We don't have any real strong evidence against Riley or anyone else—just suspicions. Am I right there?"

"You're right there," said Rider.

"So we'll arrest Riley on the whiskey charge. Get him in jail. Once we've got him, maybe we can get something more out of him. Maybe he'll break down in jail and tell us what we need to know."

They had reached the bottom of the hill, and the jail was just ahead. George was puffing from talking so much and walking at the same time.

"Or maybe," said Rider, "someone else will get excited about Bean being in jail and be afraid that ole Bean might have said something out of turn."

"You mean Omer Lyons. You think that Riley is working for Lyons. Right?"

"You're right with me, George," said Rider. "So far."

"I just saw Riley and Lyons go into Al's Eats together. They sat down together. Just as I was leaving. Just now."

"That ain't no crime," said Rider, "but it is interesting."

They had reached the jail, and Rider unlocked the front door. They went inside the building and into the office. Rider started messing with the wood stove to build up the fire for the coffeepot. George took the pot and went for water. He felt good about himself. He was thinking the same way Rider was thinking. Maybe he would make it in this police business after all. He brought the pot back in and set it on the stove. Rider had the fire going, and he took a handful of coffee grounds and dropped them into the pot of water. He moved over to his desk, sat down behind it, placed his big pistols on the desk before him, pulled out his pipe and tobacco, and began filling his pipe. Still standing by the stove, George followed Rider with his gaze.

"Rider?" he said.

"Yeah?"

"Before we heard about Mix Hail, you were tracking the whiskey sales."

"Yeah."

"You said that Riley was the one you were after, but you didn't arrest him. You didn't have any evidence."

"That's right."

Rider struck a match on the side of his desk and began puffing at his pipe.

"So how are we going to arrest him now?"

"George," said Rider, talking between puffs, "the boys ought to start gathering right about now down around the capitol. Go on down there and send them down to see me one at a time. And keep your ears open. Listen to the talk."

George looked at Rider, puzzled. He hesitated.

"Go on now," said Rider.

At the capitol, George found all of the special deputies except Beehunter. He approached Delbert Swim first.

"Delbert," he said, "run over to the office. Rider wants to talk to you."

"What about?" said Swim.

"I don't know," said George, "but it's not just you. He wants to talk to each of you—one at a time."

"Oh," said Swim, and he looked somewhat relieved. "Right now?"

"Yeah," said George. "Go ahead. I'll spell you here."

Swim took off at a trot toward the jail, and George began working his way toward the front door of the building. "Keep your ears open," Rider had said. If there was anything to be heard around the capitol at this time of morning, it would be around the front door. Two men were walking side by side toward the building. George thought that they were council members. He didn't really know all the councilmen, so he wasn't sure, but he thought they were. Elmer Lee walked around the corner of the building and up to George.

"Morning, George," he said.

"Hi, Elmer. Say. These two coming here. They council members?"

"Yeah. You send Delbert off somewhere?"

"Yeah," said George. "Rider wants to see each of you alone. When Delbert gets back, you run on down there next. Okay?"

"Okay. You know what it's about?"

"I sure don't," said George. The two council members were getting close, and George stopped talking. He put a hand on Elmer's shoulder and turned his back on the approaching legislators. He thought that they were talking Cherokee. "Listen," he whispered to Elmer Lee.

They came closer, passed by, and walked into the building.

"Did you hear what they were saying?" said George.

"Some of it," said Elmer. "It sounds like they're fixing to vote on the railroad thing this morning. They're going to vote against it. They think the railroad killed Mix."

Over Elmer Lee's shoulder, George could see Beehunter trotting up toward the square. He was late to work, so he was in a hurry. George glanced back toward the jail and saw Delbert Swim coming back. He gestured toward Swim and told Elmer Lee to go on. Swim took off, and Beehunter came trotting up. George nodded to Beehunter, then turned to wait for Swim.

"What did he want?" he asked when Swim came close.

"I don't know," said Swim. "He give me some coffee and then bullshit. That's all. I sure don't know."

George was puzzled and slightly irritated. Why couldn't Rider let him in on his little secrets? After all, he was Rider's chief deputy.

"Tell Beehunter to go on down there as soon as Elmer Lee gets back, will you?"

Swim walked over to Beehunter and started talking in Cherokee. George stared off toward the jail, an ambiguous furrow in his brow.

Chapter Seven

——

Rider stood at the window of his office looking toward the capitol. He could see the council members leaving the building, and soon he saw his deputies walking toward the jail. It's all over, he thought. One way or the other. He moved back to his chair, sat down, filled and lit his pipe. He was smoking contentedly when they came in.

"The meeting's over, Rider," said George. "Council's adjourned. They voted down the railroad. Apparently everyone thinks that the railroad lobby is responsible for the murder of Mix Hail, and that swung the vote against them."

Rider nodded and puffed his pipe. He reached into a desk drawer and took out some money, which he divided into five equal portions. Then he opened a ledger book and turned it around on the desktop to face the deputies.

"Sign your names and take your pay," he said. *"Wado."*

In a few minutes the deputies were gone—all except George Tanner. George sat on the edge of his desk, his arms folded across his chest, and he stared at Rider. Suddenly he became aware of what he was doing and remembered the inherent cultural rudeness of the act. He was ashamed of himself, and he looked down at the floor before he spoke.

"Rider," he said, "what the hell are you up to?"

Beehunter walked down Muskogee Avenue, holding his pay out in front of himself and smiling. He spoke to everyone he passed on the street, and he waved and gestured toward them with his money showing in his hand. By the time he had turned off the main street and headed toward the east edge of town, just about everyone in Tahlequah knew that Beehunter had been paid and that he was in a very good mood. About a half mile out of town, Beehunter came to a small frame house badly in need of paint. As he approached the house he called out in a loud and friendly voice.

"'Siyo. 'Siyo."

The door opened just a crack, enough for someone inside to peek out to see who was coming. Then it was opened further and a woman stood in the doorway. She spoke to Beehunter in Cherokee.

"Hello," she said. "How are you?"

"I'm fine," Beehunter answered. "Where is your old man?"

"He's coming, I think."

The woman stepped back and disappeared again into the house, but in less than a minute, Tom Spike Buck appeared in the doorway. He looked at Beehunter suspiciously for a few seconds then he stepped outside.

"What are you doing, Beehunter?" he said in Cherokee.

"I came looking for you, old friend. Look. I got paid for my work. The meeting's over and I'm free again. I need to celebrate."

"How are you going to celebrate?" said Buck.

Beehunter stuffed the money into a shirt pocket and eyed Buck coyly.

"You got a drink on you?" he asked.

"No," said Buck. "I don't have any. I know where to get some, but I don't have any money either."

"I got money," said Beehunter, and he patted the pocket into which he had stuffed his pay. "Right here."

"You work for Rider," said Buck.

"Not any more. The meeting's over. Rider just hires some of us extra just long enough for the meeting. We're not real deputies. His real deputy is that new one. Little white boy."

Beehunter laughed at his own joke, but Tom Spike Buck maintained the same sullen expression on his face. Beehunter shrugged and turned to leave.

"Ah, well," he said, "I got to go. I'll see you sometime."

"Where you going?" said Buck.

Beehunter kept walking away from Buck's house.

"Going to find somebody with a drink," he said.

Buck trotted after Beehunter and moved up beside him.

"Come on," he said. "I know where to go."

"George," said Rider, "let's go get us some dinner. You're making me nervous pacing around like that."

"It's early," said George.

"What time is it?"

George pulled out his watch and gave it a glance.

"Oh," he said. "Well, it's about a quarter of twelve. It's later than I thought."

"Come on," said Rider, and he walked out of the office without looking back. George followed him, almost angry. They walked up the hill to Rider's house without speaking. Exie gave them each a cup of coffee to keep them occupied while she finished putting the noon meal on the table. The children were at school. Rider's small talk at the table annoyed George, but he tried not to show it for Exie's sake. When the meal was done, George thanked Exie and excused himself. He walked out to the dog run and paced until Rider came out to join him. Then he started to walk toward the road, but Rider had gone to his chair. He sat down and started to load his pipe.

"Are we going back to the office?" said George, the irritation showing through in his voice.

"In a while," said Rider. "Ain't no hurry. Sit down and relax."

George sat down, but he didn't relax. He glanced at Rider, then looked away again.

"Rider," he said, "are we going to arrest Riley or not?"

"What would we arrest him for?" said Rider.

"Selling whiskey, I guess. Isn't that what you said?"

Rider sent a large cloud of blue smoke drifting up over his head.

"I said we'd get back to work on that case. We don't have any evidence on ole Bean yet. We can't arrest the man on just my suspicion, now, can we?"

"So why are we just sitting here? Why aren't we out looking—for evidence?"

"Where would we look, George?"

"Well, I don't know."

"Just calm down," said Rider. "We'll stroll on back down to the office here in a little bit and wait there. I got something going. We'll have him before the day's out."

Beehunter was broke, and he was a bit unsteady on his feet. He felt light-headed and dizzy as he weaved his way down Muskogee Avenue. He bumped into a wall, avoiding a passing lady. The lady stopped and turned to watch him stagger on, her expression clearly one of stern disapproval. Finally, Beehunter could see the jail. He took a deep breath and aimed himself carefully, then began walking toward it with a slight list to his left. He hoped that Rider was still there. He had no idea of the time. When he reached the office inside the jail, he shoved too hard on the door and almost fell into the room. He caught his balance and straightened himself up, facing Rider.

"I'm drunk," he said to Rider in Cherokee.

Rider got up and moved around the desk. He pulled a chair across the room and placed it behind Beehunter, then took Beehunter by the shoulders to help him.

"Sit down," he said.

Beehunter dropped heavily into the chair, and Rider stepped around in front of him.

"Where'd you get it?" he asked.

"Tom Spike Buck got it for me first. He wouldn't say where. Made me wait for him. So I had to drink with him. Then we got a little drunk and ran out. He didn't care so much then, and I went with him. We bought it from Bean Riley."

George couldn't understand the Cherokee conversation, but he did catch the word *tuya*, bean, and he began to understand what was going on. At least he thought that he did. He sat quietly in his chair and listened carefully for any other words he might understand, but he knew that he would have to wait for Rider's explanation.

"Where does he keep it?" said Rider.

"The springhouse."

"Good work, Beehunter."

"Go-Ahead," said Beehunter, "I feel kind of funny."

"Go find you a comfortable bed in a cell and sleep it off. You'll be all right."

Beehunter rose uneasily to his feet and began to slowly turn toward the door. Rider took hold of him by an arm and glanced over his shoulder toward George.

"George," he said, switching to English, "help Beehunter to a cell."

As George, supporting Beehunter, went through the office door leading to the cells, Rider called out after him, "But don't lock the door on him." Then he stepped over to his desk and picked up his two Colts. He pushed the six-guns into the waistband of his trousers and went to the hatrack to get his hat. George came back into the office.

"Inena," said Rider. "Come on. Let's go."

They stopped by the capitol and picked up a search warrant from Harm Boley, then walked on down to Riley's hotel. Riley was behind the counter.

"Well, well," he said as the two lawmen stepped into the lobby. "More questions?"

"Nope," said Rider. He walked over to the counter and slapped the paper down. "Read this, Bean."

Riley picked up the paper, unfolded it, and began to read. His eyes narrowed and his brow furrowed.

"What the hell you looking for?" he asked. His lips twisted and the lower one quivered slightly as he spoke.

"Whiskey," said Rider. "Let's go."

Rider pushed Bean Riley ahead of him as he walked through the hotel to the back door, then outside. George followed. They walked on across the open yard behind the building, going east toward the creek.

"Where are we going?" said Riley, his voice now indicating panic.

"Keep walking."

The springhouse was built of native stone hewn into slabs. It was down the bank and over the creek. Four stone steps led the way down to the doorway. The floor was smooth stone, but at the northeast corner of the small building was an opening that allowed the creek water to flow into the structure, run through a trench along the east wall, then along the south wall and out another opening at the southwest corner. The last of Riley's winter ice had long since melted, but it was still incredibly cool in the springhouse. And there was the whiskey. Jugs sat on the floor and in the stone recesses in the walls. Bottles filled stacked crates. Nearby were kegs of beer. Riley was sweating in the cool air inside the springhouse. He glanced toward the small door, but the doorway was filled with the form of George Tanner.

"You're under arrest, Bean," said Rider.

"Ah, hell," said Riley, "Fifty dollar fine. What the hell."

The quaver in his voice, the cold sweat, and Riley's obvious general nervousness were in sharp contrast to the indifference expressed by his words.

"Yeah," said Rider. "Fifty dollars. I guess you can handle that all right. Course, we also smash all this. How much you got tied up in your inventory here, Bean? Huh? You lose that, too."

Riley was beginning to breathe heavily. He looked from Rider to Tanner, and he fidgeted on his feet.

"Do we start smashing, Rider?" asked George.

"No hurry, George," said Rider. "Nah. There's plenty of time for that. Ole Bean here is taking this awful hard. I expect he's going to lose a bundle."

"You want me to take him on down to the jail?"

"No," said Rider. "Not yet. There's more."

"More?" said George. This time he knew what Rider was doing, and he was taking part in the game. It was a cat-and-mouse game, with Bean Riley playing the part of the tormented mouse. Only Bean wasn't playing.

"What do you mean, more?" he said. "What the hell you talking about?"

Rider looked down at his feet. With his right foot he pushed at the thin bed of straw that covered the stone floor.

"What do you see, George?" he said.

"Straw, Rider. This place is covered with straw."

"Straw?" said Riley. "So what? What are you getting at? Come on. Let's go to the damn jailhouse. I'm ready. You caught me. All right? I been selling booze. So take me to the jailhouse. Let's go."

Rider knelt and brushed away some dirt on the floor with a hand. The stone beneath his hand was stained with something dark, and so were the bits of straw which more or less covered it.

"Gi-ga," said Rider.

"What?" said Riley. "Blood?"

Rider, still kneeling, looked up at Riley. Slowly he nodded his head affirmatively.

"I, uh, I had some hog meat in here. It's gone now. Hog meat."

Rider stood up and took two steps over to the southwest corner of the springhouse. Then he knelt again and reached down into the trench. A hat was there. It had fallen into the stream of water that ran through the building, but it had washed into the corner and had lodged there rather than being washed out through the opening. Bean Riley had probably not noticed it because of the nearby stacks of whiskey cartons. Rider picked up the hat. It had a flat, medium width brim and a low, round crown. It had been darkened in the water, but it was obviously a light tan color.

Bean Riley yelled, turned, and shoved George hard against the chest with both his hands. The suddenness of Riley's action caught George by surprise, and he staggered backward out of the door and slipped on the stones, falling sideways into the creek. Riley ran up the stairs, but Rider was close behind him. Riley had made only a few strides toward his hotel when the sheriff's hands gripped him hard from behind on the shoulders. He started to turn and swing a right, but Rider took advantage of the motion and flung him forward. Riley landed sprawling on the rough ground. He started to scramble to his feet, but there before him stood George Tanner, dripping from his fall in the creek, the Starr revolver in his right hand pointed at Riley.

"That's all," said George.

"Get up," said Rider.

Riley got slowly up on his feet. He was facing George, and Rider stood behind him. His body sagged. He had given up.

"George," said Rider, "I'll take ole Bean on down to the jail. You stay here and watch over this springhouse till I get back."

Rider took Bean Riley to the jail and locked him in an upstairs cell. Beehunter was asleep in an unlocked cell downstairs. Rider didn't bother him. He would learn about the success of his undercover mission later, and Rider would question Riley later. He was convinced that Riley had been working for Omer Lyons, who in turn was employed by the railroad interests, and he wanted to get everyone who had been involved in the murder of Mix Hail. But all that could be dealt with later. He walked back to the capitol and found Harm Boley.

"We found what we were looking for, Judge," he said, "but I'd like for you to come along with me and see the evidence before anything happens to mess it up. I've got George down there right now watching it."

Boley went with Rider to the springhouse. He saw the whiskey and beer, and he saw the straw, the bloodstain, and the hat.

"I don't know yet if ole Bean actually pulled the trigger or if someone else done that," said Rider, "but he sure was involved."

"I'd say so," said Boley.

"Mix Hail and Jess Halfbreed."

"You're pretty sure the two are connected?" asked Boley.

"No question, Judge," said Rider. "Can we go ahead now and bust up these jugs?"

"Go ahead," said Boley.

"Smash them all, George," said Rider. "Then go on home and get yourself into some clean, dry clothes. I'll be at the office."

By the time George got back to the office, Rider had made a fresh pot of coffee, and Beehunter had revived somewhat from his stupor. Beehunter was sitting in the office sipping coffee, and Rider was talking to him in Cherokee. George poured himself a cup of coffee and sat at his desk.

"I was just telling Beehunter what a good job he did for us," said Rider.

"Yeah," said George, and he smiled and nodded at Beehunter, wishing he could communicate more directly with the man.

"Beehunter don't usually drink," said Rider. "I guess I gave him a pretty tough assignment."

"I guess so," said George.

"You know," said Rider, "we solved another little mystery out there today."

George looked up from his cup, a puzzled expression on his face. Something else? Had he missed something else that Rider had seen?

Was Rider always going to be at least one step ahead of him? Damn it, he thought. He was irritated at himself. He had seen the same things. He tried to think back, to picture everything in the springhouse. What could it be?

"We found out who was selling the whiskey," he said. "That was one thing. We also found out that Mix Hail's body had been kept in the springhouse, and that means that Bean Riley was involved in the murder—in both murders. What else?"

"The time element, George," said Rider. "Remember? Mix disappeared one day. We found his body the next day. Seemed like he hadn't been dead all that long. Where was he in between?"

George's eyes suddenly opened wider. He opened his mouth to speak, hesitated an instant, then said, "The springhouse. It's so cool in there. They killed him, then kept him in the springhouse until the next day, when they moved him out there on the road."

"That's it," said Rider.

Chapter Eight

George was sitting at his desk, the Starr revolver with its holster and belt lying on the desk before him. He had a cup of coffee in his hand, about half finished. The coffee in the pot on the stove was low, and George was thinking about making a fresh pot. Since the Council had adjourned and the council members had all gone home to their respective districts, the special deputies had also been dismissed. Rider had gone to the capitol to talk to the chief, and George had been left on duty at the jail.

There was nothing much to do. Bean Riley was the lone prisoner. The paperwork was all caught up. George knew that Rider planned to question Riley later on in the day, although they had already questioned the man briefly. They had implied that they knew that he had done the murders either for or with Omer Lyons. They had told him that he would surely hang for his part in the grizzly affair, and that, the vote of the Council having gone against the railroad, it had all been for naught.

Yet nothing fazed Riley. He was still nervous, anxious, obviously worried about his future, yet he said nothing to implicate Lyons or anyone else and stoutly maintained his own innocence. He swore that the bloodstain in the springhouse had resulted from fresh hog meat, which had long since been eaten, and he said that Mix Hail had come to him on the day of his disappearance to purchase whiskey. When Rider had said that he knew Mix Hail and Mix Hail did not drink, Riley had said, "That just shows what you know." Mix, Riley had said, must have dropped his hat on that occasion. Riley had not noticed at the time, but come to think of it, he had said, he did seem to recall Mix Hail walking away hatless. Yes. He was sure of that.

Rider had not given up. He was going to question Riley further, but until that time came or until Rider gave George further instructions, George really had nothing to do except sit in the office and wait. He swallowed the rest of his coffee and made a face. It had gotten cold. He got up to put on a fresh pot. He had refilled the pot and dumped the grounds into the water and was just stoking the fire when he heard someone come in at the door. He looked over his shoulder to see Lee Hunt walk into the office.

"Oh," he said. "Hello, Miss Hunt."

"Hello," she said.

George moved rapidly to place a chair for her near his desk. "Please sit down," he said.

She took the chair and thanked him.

"I just put on fresh coffee," he said. "It'll be ready soon."

"Oh, that's all right. I can really only stay a minute."

"Well," said George, "what, uh, what can I do for you?"

"I was just wondering if there was anything you wanted me to sign. You know, some kind of statement about what I saw."

"I don't know. Rider hasn't said anything. I guess if there is, we'll let you know. I don't think it's anything you need to be concerned about. But thank you for stopping by. You've already been a big help to us on this investigation."

George nervously got up and checked the coffee. Of course it wasn't ready yet. The water wasn't even boiling. Lee Hunt stood up and turned toward the door.

"Miss Hunt," said George. Then he paused. He didn't have anything to say. He felt foolish.

"Mr. Tanner," she said. "I'll make a bargain with you."

"Yes?"

"I'll call you George if you'll call me Lee."

"All right."

"There is one other reason I stopped by."

George just looked at her, waiting for her to say more.

"I came to invite you over for supper tonight. That is, if you're free."

"Oh," said George.

"Please don't feel obligated. If you have something else to do, it's all right. I realize that I haven't given you much time."

"Oh, no," said George. "I'll be there. Thank you. It's just that I'm surprised. I wasn't expecting such a—welcome invitation. I'll bring some of my books. Some of the new ones I brought from the East. If you'd like."

"I'd like that very much," said Lee. "About six?"

"Six is fine."

Lee Hunt left the office, and George stared after her for a long moment. He could scarcely believe his good fortune. He had been wondering how he could approach her, and she had come to him. Of course, he thought, her interest might be purely literary. She was an educated woman, a teacher, and he was recently returned from college in the East with some of the latest books. He could understand that. He would have to be careful. If that was the only interest she had in him, he would certainly honor and respect that. But he hoped and longed to find out that her interest would go beyond that. George felt like shouting out his joy, then he heard the water behind him boiling rapidly. He turned quickly and moved the pot over so that it was not directly above the fire. Then he heard Riley shouting from his cell.

"Hey, Rider. Rider, come here. Come in here, damn it."

George stepped through the door into the hallway that led to the cells.

"Rider's out," he yelled. "Quiet down."

"Well, where the hell is he?"

"You don't need to know where he is," said George. "Just shut up."

"Come here. Is that you, deputy? What's your name? Tanner, is it?"

"It's Tanner," said George. He stepped further into the hallway. "What do you want?"

"My throat's dry," said Riley. "I need a drink."

"Of water?"

"Yeah, water. I know you got nothing else. Wouldn't give it to me if you did. A man's got a right to a drink of water, ain't he? Even in jail?"

George walked on down to the cell, and he pointed to a bucket in a corner behind Riley.

"You've got water, Riley," he said. "There's a whole bucket of water, and it's fresh."

Riley turned toward the bucket, took a couple of long strides, and kicked it over, spilling water over the cell floor and out into the hallway.

"This?" he said. "It stinks. I want some fresh water."

"Damn you, Riley," said George. "You're going to mop that up, and if you want anymore, you'd damn well better quiet down."

George stalked down the hall, got a mop and the cell keys, and went back to Riley's cell.

"Bring me that bucket," he said. "Get it."

Riley picked up the bucket.

"Put it here by the door."

Riley dropped the bucket by the cell door.

"Now get back over there against the wall," said George.

Riley backed up to the far wall, and George unlocked the cell door. He swung the door open, tossed the mop inside, and reached for the bucket. Riley produced a Colt .45 from somewhere, cocked back the hammer, and then aimed the gun at George in one sweeping motion.

"Don't move, you son of a bitch," he said.

George was caught bent over, reaching for the bucket. He stayed that way, his eyes on the barrel of the .45 that was pointing right at his face. Riley began working his way around the cell, keeping to the wall.

"Get in here," he said, and he gestured with his revolver toward the wall opposite the one against which he was creeping. George slowly straightened himself up and stepped into the cell.

"Go on," shouted Riley. George stepped in further, and Riley got quickly out the door. He slammed the door shut and locked it, removed the keys, and rushed down the hallway. At the end of the hallway, he stopped and looked back toward the cell.

"I ought to kill you," he shouted. Then he was gone. George banged the heels of his hands against his forehead.

"Oh, no," he said. "Damn."

He had been suckered. His prisoner was gone, and he was in the cell, locked up tight. It was humiliating. It would be even worse when Rider got back. Damn, he thought. What will I tell Rider? What can I tell him? He dropped heavily onto the cot in the cell to wait.

Outside the front door of the jail, Bean Riley stopped. Probably everyone in town knew that he had been arrested. He couldn't afford to be seen. And Rider had made him change his trousers for those damned striped ones. Even if he was too far away to be recognized, people would see those damned stripes. He thought about going back inside to find his own trousers, but he couldn't bring himself to do that. He was out of the jail, and he didn't want to go back in. But those stripes. He would have liked to kill Rider, but Rider wasn't around. He would have killed that damned deputy, but the shot would have attracted attention. He was glad of the tall board fence running around the jail, but he had to do something. Rider would come back sooner or later. He couldn't simply stand there in the jail yard.

There were horses and saddles in the sheriff's barn. He could probably make his way there without being seen—if he was careful. He started to make his way around the building. He felt a lump in his throat when he passed by the gallows out back. Finally he reached the barn, and he rushed inside. He grabbed the first saddle he came to and threw it on the back of the first horse. Then he climbed into the saddle and raced away from town, heading south. He saw a wagon coming toward him and panicked momentarily. He jerked the reins of his mount to the right and rode down into the field and toward the woods. The driver of the wagon, a black woodcutter, hauled back on his reins.

"Hey," he shouted. His eyes opened wide as he stared after the rider in the striped pants who was racing toward the woods.

"Hey."

"Don't feel bad, George," Rider was saying. "It could have happened to me. No way you could have known that ole Bean had a gun in there. You done the right thing. If a man's got a gun on you, do what he says. Now run on and get us a couple of horses saddled. We'll try to find out which way he went."

George almost ran into a black man as he hurried out the front door of the jail. The man stepped aside, then entered the building and made his way to the office.

"Hello, Go-Ahead," he said.

Rider turned away from the cabinet from which he was gathering ammunition to see who had come in.

"Hello, Isaac," he said. "Sorry. I'm in a hurry. Just had a prisoner escape on us."

"I know," said Isaac. "I seen him."

Rider stopped what he was doing to give Isaac his full attention.

"Where?" he said.

"Man on a horse wearing striped britches," said Isaac. "Just on the edge of town. He was headed south on the road, but when he seen me headed towards him, he turned west off the road. Headed into the trees off to the west. I think he had a gun in his hand. Six-gun."

"Good, Isaac," said Rider, slapping the woodcutter on the shoulder. He turned to stuff the bullets he had been gathering into his vest pockets. "Thanks for stopping in. Have a cup of coffee. I got to go."

Rider ran out of the building and toward the barn, but George was already on his way back with the horses. Rider took the reins of one from George and swung into the saddle.

"Inena," he said, and he kicked the horse in the sides and started riding south. George mounted up and followed. They rode hard just a little ways out of town, then Rider slowed his mount to a walk. Then he halted. George did the same. Rider looked off to his right. Not more than a hundred yards across a field, a hollow ran more or less parallel with the road. On the other side of the hollow, a large hill rose sharply and abruptly. The thick growth of brush and trees that covered the hill began in the hollow.

"What is it?" said George.

Rider shook his head and made a quick gesture with his hand to indicate silence.

"He's off over there somewhere," he said.

They sat still in their saddles for another long moment, looking off across the field and listening. George's horse snorted and shook his head. Rider turned his mount toward the field and urged it forward at a slow walk.

"Come on," he said.

They rode slowly off the road and into the tall grass of the field, heading for the draw at the foot of the hill. As they rode they gradually increased the distance between them. There was a sudden noise up ahead, a heavy, frantic scurrying sound, followed by a motion visible to them. It was Bean Riley lashing at his stolen horse, trying to ride up the far side of the draw. The thickness of the brush and the looseness of the rocky ground on the steep incline were too much for the horse, and it slipped back down. Riley half fell, half climbed, out of the saddle. Gun in hand, he scampered up the side of the draw and ran into the thicket at the base of the hill. Rider kicked the sides of his horse and hurried across the field. George was close behind. Near the edge of the draw, they stopped and dismounted. Riley's abandoned mount was fidgeting around down in the draw. Rider pointed forward and off to his left. George understood. They would try to close in on Riley from both sides. As Rider moved off to his right and started down into the draw, George moved left.

George hit loose rock with his first step down and slid on his backside the rest of the way down into the draw. He was bruised, but the worst thing about it was the embarrassment. He knew that no one saw him, but he also knew that his slide had made considerable noise. He got to his feet and picked his way across the draw through the thick undergrowth and began making his way cautiously up the other side. He came out slowly, half expecting Riley to be waiting up there somewhere to take a shot at him. There was no shot. He could see no sign of either Riley or Rider. He moved into the woods on the hillside. He hesitated for a moment, looking around and listening. He might as well have been off somewhere alone. He started forward again, and somewhere above him a blue jay screamed angrily at him. He flinched, stopped again, and then pulled the Starr out of its holster. The ground was getting steeper. He climbed slowly. A low branch scraped across his face. The brush was getting thicker. If he watched the ground to keep from stumbling, he found his arms tangled or his face slapped. It was slow, tough going, and somewhere up there was Bean Riley, desperate and armed.

George was sweating, and he suddenly realized that he was cold. It must be the shade in the thick woods, he thought. But no. It was darker all of a sudden. He looked up, searching through the heavy overhead canopy of branches for the sky, and where he caught glimpses of it, it had turned dark. Heavy black thunderclouds had moved in, causing a sharp drop in temperature. Soon it would rain—a heavy rain. They had to find Riley soon. There was a flash in the dark sky, followed soon after by a loud clap of thunder. Then there was a shot. It sounded from off to George's right. It must have been Riley who had fired, he figured. Rider would never have fired first at the fugitive without warning. He crouched behind a thick oak tree and strained his eyes, trying to see something through the trees.

"Rider?" he called. Then he heard Rider's voice, but it was not in answer to his call.

"Bean, this is Rider. Did you hear that other voice? That was my deputy over there on the other side. We're on both sides of you, Bean. Give it up. We don't want to have to kill you."

George heard another shot, and it was followed quickly by Riley's voice.

"You don't want to kill me, huh? You just want to save me to hang. You go to hell. Both of you."

"Bean, you'll get a trial," said Rider.

A third shot sounded. George thought that all three shots had been fired by Riley, but he couldn't be certain. A heavy drop of rain splattered on his forehead. He stood upright and started slowly toward the direction of the gunshot sounds. Then he heard a crashing through the woods. It's Riley, he thought, coming at me, attacking the weakest point. The heavy raindrops started falling faster. George hurried ahead toward another large tree trunk, but he stepped on wet leaves that had been covering slick rock, and he fell heavily on his back. His breath was knocked out of him, but he managed to hold on to the Starr revolver.

Suddenly Riley was looming over him. Riley hesitated an instant, apparently as startled by the sight of George flat on the ground as George was by the other's sudden appearance. Then Riley raised his pistol and aimed it at George. He started to thumb back the hammer. George was still out of breath. He wanted to tell Riley not to try it, but he couldn't speak. He saw the gun moving, leveling at him, saw the thumb on the hammer. He raised the Starr and pulled the trigger, and he heard the loud report, saw the red hole appear in the center of Riley's chest, saw Riley jerk backward a little, a look of surprise on his face, watched as Riley's knees began to buckle and his fingers went limp. Riley dropped to his knees, then fell over on his back. It became incredibly quiet and still except for the big raindrops falling and for the loud ringing in George's ears.

"Ah," said George, "damn. Damn."

Chapter Nine

"Have another cup of coffee, George, and stop blaming yourself," said Rider.

"But he's all we had," said George. "We're right back where we started."

Rider walked over to George's desk, picked up the cup, and refilled it with coffee. He placed the cup back on the desk in front of George and took the pot back to the stove.

"I don't like it anymore than you do," he said, "but it's done, and we just have to deal with things as they are. George, if I'd been flat on my back and ole Bean had aimed at me, I'd have damn sure shot him dead myself. Much as I wanted him here alive, I'd have shot him dead. I'd lots rather have dragged his body down out of them woods than yours. Okay? I don't want to hear no more whining about how you messed things up. Ole Bean done it all himself."

George sipped at his coffee. His head was beginning to clear a little. It wasn't just that he had killed the only man they had who might have given them more information. It was more than that. He had never killed a man before, and it had given George an uncomfortable, almost sick feeling. He couldn't tell that to Rider. But his ears had stopped ringing, and he was starting to think more clearly.

"He didn't get that gun in his cell all by himself," he said.

"You're right about that, George," said Rider. "Omer Lyons got that to him somehow. I know it. Lyons is behind it all, but I can't think how to prove it. I just can't think how."

"Miss Hunt came by the office this afternoon," said George.

"Oh, yeah?"

"She, uh, she invited me to have supper with her tonight."

"You didn't turn her down, did you?" asked Rider.

"No. I said I'd be there. I guess I will."

"Well, why don't you run on to the house and get yourself cleaned up. We'll call it a day. Go on. I'll shut down here and be along in a while."

George pulled on an old slicker that had been hanging in the office, and, ducking his head, went out into the rain.

Rider poured himself another cup of coffee and sat back down. George will be all right, he thought. He's feeling pretty bad right now because he thinks that it's all his fault that ole Bean got out of jail and then got killed. He'll come out of it. Going to see Miss Hunt tonight will help. Yes, indeed. He slurped at his coffee. It was too hot to gulp.

He thought about Omer Lyons. There was no way he could figure to prove any connection between Lyons and Riley, especially now that Riley was dead. Before that unfortunate event occurred, Rider had thought that he might sweat the information out of Riley. Now, as George had said, they were right back where they started. I'll just have to dog Lyons's trail, he thought. Just keep nipping at his heels. See if I can't make him slip up, give himself away.

Then he decided that he might as well get started. He took one more slurp of coffee, stood up, picked up the Colts from his desktop, and tucked them into his waistband. He moved across the room to the wall pegs where his hat was hanging, as was another old slicker, and he put those on and walked outside, locking the door behind him.

At the Capital Hotel, Rider found Troy Anglin behind the counter. Anglin was a young man, a halfbreed no more than twenty, who sometimes worked for Riley. Rider knew his family and knew that they were related to the Rileys. Young Anglin had apparently taken over the duties at the hotel following Riley's arrest.

"'*Siyo*, Troy," said Rider. He stopped just inside the door and shook the water off his hat and slicker.

"Hi, Go-Ahead," said Anglin. "If you come to tell me about Bean, we already heard. You all killed him. I guess you had to."

"He didn't give us no choice, Troy. George Tanner actually did the killing. If he hadn't, ole Bean would have killed him. News travels fast."

"Well," said Anglin, "you bring a dead man into town, it don't take long for the news to get just three blocks down the street."

"More like five blocks," said Rider.

"Well, whatever."

"What's going to happen now with the hotel?"

"I'm not sure. I guess I'll hang on here and run it for a while and just kind of wait and see. Bean had a wife once, I guess, but she run off some time ago, and they didn't have no kids. He's got a brother somewhere down in Canadian District. That's what I've heard. Maybe he'll come up here and take it over. I don't know. But there's people staying here, and someone's got to look after the place."

"Well, we'll try to get word down to his brother and get this thing settled one way or another. You see if you can find out for me what the brother's name is and where I can get ahold of him. You do that?"

"Yeah. I think so."

"Is Omer Lyons still here?"

"Yeah," said Anglin. "I think he's up in his room right now. He's in number three."

"Thanks, Troy." Rider pulled off the slicker and hung it on a coatrack in the corner of the lobby. Then he walked down the hall to room number three. He knocked on the door.

"Who is it?" came Lyons's voice from behind the door.

"It's Go-Ahead Rider. I want to talk to you."

There was a pause, then Lyons jerked the door open.

"What do you want?" he said.

"Can I come in?" said Rider.

"I'd rather you didn't."

Rider shoved Lyons to one side and walked into the room. There was an open suitcase, half packed, lying on the bed.

"I won't stay long," said Rider. "I wondered if you'd be staying around any longer. The railroad boys probably took you off their payroll after the vote went bad for you. That right?"

Lyons didn't answer. He stood back against the wall, his arms folded across his chest, and glared at Rider.

"And, uh, your partner got himself killed while ago. You hear about that?"

"What partner?" said Lyons. "I didn't have no partner. You talking about Riley? Partner in what? My job was talking to council members. Trying to convince them that the railroad would be good for Tahlequah. Just talking. I didn't have no partner."

Rider stared at Lyons. Lyons shifted his weight nervously, then paced across the room.

"I know you killed Riley," he said, "but he wasn't my partner. What the hell you kill him for, anyway?"

"Well," said Rider, "I arrested old Bean for the murder of Mix Hail. I had pretty good evidence, too. The charge would have stuck. He'd have been found guilty. And I think he killed Jess Halfbreed, too, but I didn't charge him with that one, just only with ole Mix. The only thing is, ole Bean didn't have no reason to kill ole Mix, not that I know about, he didn't. Not unless he done it for someone else. Maybe someone he was working for."

"Wait a minute," said Lyons.

"Now you had a reason to want ole Mix out of the way," said Rider. "He was a strong opponent of your railroad buddies. He was influential on the Council. He could swing a few votes one way or the other if he took a mind to."

"Damn it, Rider."

"It come to me that you might have hired poor ole Bean. You know, he wasn't too damn smart. It come to me that he might have been working for you, and that would explain why he killed them two. That makes sense."

"It ain't true," said Lyons. "And you can't prove anything. You can't pin it on me. Get the hell out of here now. Get out."

Rider walked to the door. It was still standing open. He turned back toward Lyons.

"Are you leaving town?" he asked.

"None of your damn business."

Beehunter's house was not far, and Rider walked to it in the rain. It was a small log house just at the edge of the woods, barely out of town. Beehunter was at home with his wife and four children. No one in the house could speak any English, so Rider spoke to them in Cherokee. He started with small talk. They talked about the sudden rain and speculated on how long it would last and whether or not it would cause any flooding. Beehunter's wife gave Rider a cup of coffee and some bean bread to eat. He took it and nibbled at the bread, knowing that if he ate it all, she would give him more. He didn't want to eat too much, because Exie would have his supper ready when he got home. After a while, Rider began to work his way around to the point of his visit.

"You know," he said, "George killed Bean today."

"George did?" said Beehunter.

Rider explained to Beehunter how Riley had escaped, and how

he and George had pursued him, and finally how the killing had taken place.

"I think that Omer Lyons got the gun to him somehow," he said. "I think that Bean was working for Lyons. Lyons paid him to kill Mix and Jess. That's what I think about it."

"Well," said Beehunter, "you're probably right."

"I don't have any proof," said Rider. "I can't arrest Lyons on just my own suspicion, but I'm afraid he's getting ready to leave town. I can't watch him all the time either."

"You want me to watch him for you, Go-Ahead?"

That was exactly what Rider had wanted, and in typical Cherokee fashion, he had talked around the issue until Beehunter had volunteered to do the job. Finally Rider got up to leave.

"If he starts to leave town," he said, "don't try to stop him. Just find me and let me know."

Rider had one more stop to make before going home. He found Chief Ross still in his office at the capitol building, and he told the chief about Riley's arrest, escape, and death. He also told him how he believed that Lyons was involved.

"Let's go talk to Harm," said Ross.

They entered Judge Boley's office just as the judge was getting ready to leave for the day.

"I'm glad we caught you, Harm," said Ross. "We need some legal advice."

Again Rider told the whole story. Boley had heard already about the killing of Riley, but he listened patiently to the sheriff give his own account of the incident.

"Riley was the only thing we had," said Rider. "We had the evidence on him. We could have convicted him of murder. At least the murder of ole Mix. We might even have been able to prove that he killed Jess, too. But what I was hoping for was to get him to tell us about Lyons. We got no evidence against Lyons at all, and I'm damn sure he was behind all this. What I'm afraid of is that he'll leave town before we can get anything on him."

Boley paced across the floor, rubbing his chin thoughtfully. He stopped and looked at Chief Ross, then he looked at Rider.

"If Omer Lyons tries to leave town," he said, "arrest him on suspicion. We'll do what we can to get a conviction."

"All right," said Rider. "I've got a man watching him."

The rain had almost stopped by the time George arrived at Lee Hunt's house, but his slicker was dripping wet and his boots were muddy. He stood awkwardly at her front door.

"Come on in," she said.

"My boots are awful muddy," said George. "I don't want to track up your floor."

"That's what the mat's for. Come on in."

George stepped carefully inside and stood on the mat. He reached back behind himself and pushed the door closed. He looked down at his feet. The boots were so heavy with mud that it seemed a waste of effort to try to clean them.

"Can I, uh, just pull them off?" he asked.

"Of course."

George struggled out of his boots and left them on the mat. He was glad that he had washed himself and put on clean socks before leaving his room at Rider's house. He was also thankful that the socks were a good pair, ones without holes. He slipped off the slicker, and Lee Hunt took it from him and hung it on a peg in the wall by the front door. She motioned toward a big rocking chair.

"Please sit down, George," she said. "I'll have supper on in just a few minutes."

"I forgot to bring my books," said George. "I'm sorry. I thought about it when I was almost here. I just forgot."

"Oh, that's all right. I'd love to see them, but we can do that another time. You don't need to apologize."

"Well, I meant to bring them. I know you'd be interested in them. Some of them are fairly recent. It's just that I—meant to."

George still sounded as if he were apologizing, so Lee stopped what she was doing in the kitchen and stepped over to face him. She looked at him with an expression of serious concern. George thought that she looked like a mother preparing to console a hurt child.

"George," she said, "I'm just glad to see you. I really didn't know if you'd show up tonight. I think I know what's bothering you. I heard about Mr. Riley."

"Oh," said George. "Yeah. I didn't know if I should come over here tonight after that. I don't know if I'll be very good company. I—I am kind of—upset."

"Well, please try to relax. I know you were just doing your job—and protecting yourself. We'll have a pleasant meal here in a minute, and then we'll just relax and chat. And don't feel as if you have to be entertaining, either. That will be my responsibility tonight."

She poured him a cup of coffee to sip while he waited for the table to be set. Then she served him roast beef, mashed potatoes with brown gravy, green beans, and fried okra. There were also hot rolls and fresh butter. George drank a large glass of milk with his meal and more coffee afterward. And she had been right, he thought. He did feel better, more relaxed. She was wonderful, this young woman. He had thought that perhaps he shouldn't even show up for the meal after he had killed a man. He had felt somehow guilty, no longer decent, but she had accepted his deed as something done in the line of duty and had not at all been appalled by it. She was very pretty and well educated, and she was obviously concerned about his own feelings. And not the least of her attractions to George was her mild aggressiveness. She had actually invited him to have supper with her in her home rather than wait for him to make the first advance. It was rather bold of her, and he liked that. Probably her neighbors would soon be gossiping about her, if they weren't already.

"That was a wonderful meal," he said.

"Have some more. There's plenty."

"Oh, no, thank you," he said. "I can't. I'm full as a tick. Oh, excuse me."

She laughed. And George liked her laugh. It was soft and pretty but not silly, not a giggle or a titter, a soft, pretty, musical laugh. A lovely lady's laugh. She refilled his coffee cup and carried it to the small table beside the rocking chair.

"You sit here and be comfortable," she said, "while I clear the table."

"Let me help you," he said.

"No. You just sit and relax."

George walked over to the rocking chair and sat down, and Lee busied herself cleaning off the table.

"You know," George said, "I started not to show up tonight."

"I gathered that," she said, "from what you said earlier."

"I'm glad that I came."

"Me, too." She turned and looked at him and smiled. "I'm glad you came."

George took a sip of his coffee, set the cup down on the table, and got up. He walked up to Lee in the kitchen.

"I wish you'd let me help you," he said.

"I'm doing just fine."

"But I'm not. I don't feel right just sitting there and watching you work. Especially after all the work you've already done fixing this meal."

She stopped again and looked him in the face, her hands on her hips, and she raised an eyebrow at him.

"All right," she said, "if it will make you feel better. We'll have it done in no time."

When they had finished washing and drying and putting away the dishes, they sat back down, George in the rocker, Lee in a straight-back chair directly across the small room from him, and they talked. George told her how he had killed Bean Riley, how it had made him feel. He told her as well how he had felt at blame for not only Riley's death but also for his escape before that. He told her how Rider had tried to comfort him by saying that the same thing would have happened had he been there instead of George. He surprised himself by the things that he told her. She made him feel so comfortable. It seemed somehow natural to George to tell her—anything. And then he noticed the time. Again he was embarrassed. He had stayed too long. He stammered an apology and got up to leave.

"I should have watched the time more closely," he said. "I've stayed too late. I'm sorry."

"Nonsense," said Lee. "I've had a wonderful time."

George walked to the front door and bent to pick up a boot. Lee opened the front door. It was raining again—hard.

"You can't walk out in that," she said.

"Oh, I'll be all right. Besides, it might go on all night."

"Why don't you stay the night?"

George felt his face turn hot.

"Oh, no," he said. "I couldn't do that. It would—"

"Of course you can. I'll make you a nice pallet right over there on the floor. It will be all right."

Chapter Ten

"Nothing happened, Rider," said George. "She made me a pallet on the floor, and she slept in her bed. That's all."

"George, you can stop defending the lady's reputation," said Rider. "It ain't been attacked. Did I say anything?"

"Well," said George, "nothing happened."

Rider was sitting in his characteristic pose, his legs up and his feet crossed on the desktop, and he was filling his pipe. His two Colts lay on the desk in front of him.

"Pour us up some coffee, will you, George?" he said. "We've got to go down the street here in a minute and check with ole Beehunter."

"Beehunter?" said George, as he moved across the room to the coffeepot.

"I've got him watching Omer Lyons for us. The man's fixing to leave town if we let him."

George put Rider's cup on the desk beside the Colts. Then he sat on the edge of Rider's desk, his own cup in his hand. Rider scratched a match on the side of the desk and lit his pipe.

"How do we stop him if he tries to leave?" George asked.

"Arrest him. I'd rather get more evidence on him first, but I checked with the chief and the judge, and we all agreed that it'd be better to arrest him and try to convict him than to just let him ride out of here. So for right now we watch him and we hound him and we hope that he gives himself away somehow."

"He might get nervous and slip up somewhere," said George.

"He might."

Rider's smoke was beginning to gather in clouds above his head.

"She sure can cook," said George.

"What?"

"Oh. I was just thinking about Miss Hunt. She's a real fine cook, too."

"George," said Rider, "you better marry that woman before someone else does."

George's face turned slightly red, and he could feel the flush. He looked away from Rider.

"Why, I don't know her well enough for that," he said. "I just met her—really."

"She's cooked you two meals," said Rider, "and the second one was breakfast. I'd say you got pretty well acquainted in a short time."

"Rider, damn it," said George, stalking over to his own desk, "I told you that nothing like that happened over there last night."

Rider looked up at George with an expression of feigned innocence on his face.

"Like what?" he said. "What'd I say?"

"Well, anyway," said George, "I think it's too early for me to speak to her about matrimony. It—it just is."

Rider finished his coffee and stood up. His pipe was in his mouth. He picked up the two Colts and shoved them into his waistband.

"Most folks would say it's too early for her to let you spend the night in her house—in a pallet on the floor—but she did. Come on. Let's go."

"Where?" said George.

"To see Beehunter."

"Oh. Okay."

George took a last gulp of his coffee and followed Rider out the door. In a few minutes they had found Beehunter across the street from the Capital Hotel. He was standing outside, leaning against a storefront. The street was wet and muddy, but the sky was clear.

"'Siyo," said Beehunter as he saw the two lawmen approaching.

Rider leaned against the storefront beside Beehunter and began a conversation in Cherokee. George felt left out. He tried to listen, to see if he could understand any words, but he couldn't catch any. Now and then, he glanced across the street at the hotel. Finally Rider said something to Beehunter, and Beehunter nodded, stood up straight, turned, and walked off down the street.

"I told him we'd spell him for a while. Let him get a bite to eat and a catnap. He said Lyons has gone out to eat once, and he's gone in and out a couple other times. Never stayed out long. He thinks that Lyons knows we're watching him."

"Is that good or bad?" asked George.

"I'd just as soon he knew about it," said Rider. "Make him nervous. Stay here. I'll be right back."

Rider went inside the store and soon reemerged with two straight-back, cane-bottomed chairs. He placed them on the wooden sidewalk, pushing them back against the storefront.

"We might as well be comfortable," he said, and he took out his pipe and tobacco pouch. George sat down beside him.

Omer Lyons came out of his room and walked to the hotel lobby. He hesitated as he passed by the front desk, as if he wanted to say something to Anglin, then stalked across the lobby to the big window in the front wall.

"Anything I can do for you, Mr. Lyons?" said Anglin.

"No," said Lyons. He leaned against the wall just to the side of the window and tried to peer outside without being seen. Across the street the two lawmen sat on the sidewalk, watching the front of the hotel. They couldn't stop him from leaving, he thought. They had no evidence against him. He was a free man. He could come and go as he pleased. But why were they watching him like that? What did they think they were going to do if he headed out of town? Damn them, anyway. Damn them both. He should have had Riley take care of both of them right at the beginning. Then maybe everything would have worked out all right. He would have gotten a big bonus from the railroad company had the vote gone the other way. But now he had to get out of Tahlequah, out of the Cherokee Nation. They didn't have anything on him, he kept assuring himself, but what if—what if there was something he had overlooked? What could it be? Of course, there was nothing.

Rider was just trying to run a bluff on him. He was sure of that. God damn that Rider. He was just sitting there across the street, calmly puffing on his pipe. Lyons wondered briefly whether or not he could hit Rider and Tanner with pistol shots from where he stood before either one of them could react. It was unlikely, and he dismissed the thought almost as soon as it had occurred to him. But what would he do? Suddenly he turned and walked to the desk. He pulled his wallet out of the inside pocket of his coat and took out some bills.

"Here," he said. "I'm paying up. I'll be out of here in the morning."

He paid Anglin and went back to his room. His suitcase was already packed. He knew that a stagecoach would leave Tahlequah in the morning for Fort Gibson. He would take that. He didn't know where he would go from there. Arkansas? Texas? He would decide later. The important thing was to just get out, get away to safety. Maybe he would even change his name. He wanted a drink of whiskey real bad, but he had no idea where to go for one. Riley's stock had been destroyed, and besides he didn't know if he could trust Anglin with such a request. And it wouldn't be safe to go out looking for booze. If Rider caught him, that would just give the sheriff a good excuse to arrest him. He would have to wait until he got to someplace where liquor was legal. It was going to be a long wait. A long day and night. He stretched out on the bed and stared at the ceiling.

Judge Harm Boley was walking down the sidewalk with two strangers. Rider saw them coming. He gave them only a cursory glance, but he noted that the two men with Boley were both well dressed. They were white men, he was pretty sure. Of course, it was sometimes impossible to tell some of the mixed-blood Cherokees from whites just by their appearance, but Rider knew most of the local breeds, particularly the prominent ones, and he had never seen these two men before. Therefore he reasoned that they were white men. *Yonegs.* When they came closer, Rider stood up. So did George.

"'*Siyo,* Judge," he said.

"Rider," said Boley, "I have two gentlemen here with me who want to meet you. Gentlemen, this is Sheriff Go-Ahead Rider. And this is his deputy, Mr. George Tanner. Rider, George, this is Harvey Masters, and with him here is Charles Wainwright. They've come down from St. Louis to represent the railroad company."

"Pleased to meet you, Sheriff Rider, Mr. Tanner," said Wainwright, extending his hand. "We're here to cooperate with you any way we can. As we've already explained to Judge Boley, we hired Mr. Lyons to represent our interests as a lobbyist with your Council. We certainly never intended for his activities to go beyond those legitimately associated with that line of endeavor. We understand that there have been two murders here that seem to be connected to our interests, and we want to assure you that we are not and never have been in the business of murder. If Lyons had anything to do with those crimes, he was acting on his own. As soon as we heard of the possibility of his involvement, we terminated his employment. We'll stay in town as long as you like and answer any questions you might have concerning Lyons's brief period of employment with us."

"I see," said Rider. "Mr. Wainwright, would you accompany me back to my office? I would like to ask you some questions, and I'd like to be able to sit and make some notes while we talk."

"Certainly," said Wainwright.

"Do you want me along?" said Boley.

"No, thank you, Judge," said Rider. "I don't believe so."

"Then I'll take my leave. See you gentlemen later."

Boley turned and started down the sidewalk back toward the capitol building. Rider turned to George.

"You stay here and keep watch until Beehunter gets back. Then come on back to the office." He turned to the other railroad man. "Mister, uh—"

"Masters," said the man. "Harvey Masters."

"Yeah," said Rider. "Mr. Masters, would you mind staying here with George? You can take my seat here. You two can talk. Maybe George will think of something to ask you about that I don't. Two conversations might be better than one."

"That's fine with me," said Masters.

Inside the Capital Hotel, Lyons had gotten up and left his room again. He paced nervously back into the lobby, and he went back to the window to look out again. Across the street he saw Masters and Wainwright talking to Rider and Tanner, and he saw Wainwright walk away with Rider. He saw Masters sit down beside Tanner. The two of them were watching the front of the hotel. Damn, he thought. They're selling me down the river. He watched another minute or so, then went back to his room. Once inside, he locked the door. On the table beside the bed was a Marston three-shot .32 pocket pistol. Lyons knew that it was loaded, but he checked the load anyway. He put the pistol back on the table and sat down stiffly on the edge of the bed. God, he wanted a drink of whiskey.

Beehunter had returned to his post by the time Lyons had decided he could stand it no longer. He walked boldly out the front door of the hotel, deliberately avoiding even a glance across the street at Beehunter, and he walked quickly, heading south. Beehunter kept his seat until Lyons was about a block away. Then he stood up and began to follow. Another half block down the street, Lyons crossed over. He had not looked back to see whether or not he was being followed. Beehunter strolled along behind until Lyons went into Al's Eats. Lyons had settled himself at a table and ordered a meal when Beehunter casually entered the cafe. Lyons tried not to look at him. Beehunter sat at the counter.

"*Kawi agwaduli,*" he said.

Al knew only enough Cherokee to recognize an order, and he poured Beehunter a cup of coffee. Beehunter drank three cups. Lyons had eaten only about half his meal. He stood up angrily and stalked over to the counter, stopping beside Beehunter.

"Damn you," he shouted.

Beehunter looked up at Lyons and smiled.

"You're following me," said Lyons.

Beehunter gave a shrug.

"*Tla yi-go-li-g',*" he said.

"You son of a bitch," said Lyons.

"Hey," said Al, from behind the counter, "you going to eat or not?"

"I'm done," said Lyons.

"Then pay me and get out of here. I don't put up with no trouble in here."

Lyons fumbled in his pocket, found some money, and tossed it on the counter. Then he walked out. Beehunter calmly finished his coffee, paid his tab, and got up to follow Lyons. Lyons went back to the hotel, got into his room, and locked himself in once again.

As Lyons had anticipated, he spent a long night. He was up early. He had not undressed to sleep, and he had slept fitfully. His bag was packed, and he knew that he was ready to leave, yet he rechecked all the drawers in the room's furniture. He looked in the mirror on the wall and slicked back his hair. He checked his pocket watch. It was still early, but maybe the damn stage would be early for a change. Something had to go right, he told himself. He picked up the Marston, rechecked its load, and dropped it into a side pocket of his coat. Then he picked up his suitcase and left the room. He had paid up the day before, so he didn't have to stop by the desk for anything. The key was on the table in the room. As he headed for the front door, Anglin saw him leaving and looked up from his work.

"Good-bye, Mr. Lyons," he said.

Lyons did not answer, did not even glance in Anglin's direction. He jerked open the front door and hurried out, leaving the door to close by itself—or not.

Beehunter walked into Rider's office and spoke in Cherokee. Rider stood up from behind his desk and picked up his two Colts. As he was tucking the Colts into his waistband, he shot a glance in George's direction.

"Lyons is catching the stage," he said. "Let's go."

Beehunter poured himself a cup of coffee and watched the two others hurry out of the office. He took the coffee cup, walked around behind Rider's desk, sat down, and propped his feet up on the desktop. He took a long slurp from the cup.

"Ah," he said.

Outside Rider paused.

"All right, George," he said. "There's no hurry. Lyons must be anxious to get out of town. It's a little early yet for the stage. We'll come at him from two different directions. Move in calm and easy. I don't expect any trouble from him, but stay alert just in case. And you don't do anything—unless you see that I need some help. Got it?"

"I got it," said George.

Lyons was not sitting on the bench near where the stage would stop. He was too nervous for that. His suitcase was on the bench, but he was up and pacing back and forth on the board sidewalk. He saw the stage coming down the street, moving toward where he stood waiting, coming to take him away to safety. He picked up his bag from the bench and pushed his way ahead of the other waiting passengers so he would be the first on board. The stage came closer, and Lyons saw Go-Ahead Rider walking toward him, coming from the south. Rider didn't appear to be in any particular hurry. He was probably not going to arrest anyone, Lyons thought. He was going to try to pull his bluff again, that's all. Rider strolled closer, and the stage rolled closer, and Lyons became more nervous. He glanced to his left, and there he saw George Tanner walking toward him from the north. He thought about running. Where to? There was no place to go. He told himself again that it was nothing more than a bluff. He pulled himself up straight to await the stage. The stage lurched to a halt almost in front of Lyons, and Rider stepped up beside him.

"Going somewhere, Mr. Lyons?" said Rider.

"None of your damn business," said Lyons.

"Oh, yes it is. You're under arrest."

Lyons tried to put on his boldest appearance and manner. The worst thing, he thought, is to appear nervous, to seem guilty.

"What's the charge?" he said.

Rider reached out to pull Lyons's coat open, to see if he was armed. He didn't see a weapon, but he felt the weight on the right side of the coat. He reached for the pocket.

"Back off," said Lyons.

"You take it easy, Mr. Lyons," said George. He was standing right behind the man. Lyons's big body relaxed. The fight went out of him. His shoulders sagged, and he seemed to lose an inch or two of height.

"All right," he said. "What's the charge?" His voice was not as bold or as belligerent as it had been. Rider reached into the coat pocket and pulled out the Marston .32. He held it up for Lyons, George, and the nearby witnesses to see.

"How about carrying a concealed weapon for starters?" he said. "Come on. Let's go to the jailhouse."

Chapter Eleven

"Gentlemen of the jury," said Judge Boley, "have you reached a verdict?"

In the jury box, the foreman of the jury stood up and faced the judge.

"Yes, we have, your honor," he said.

The courtroom was silent. Lyons sat beside his attorney, beads of perspiration on his forehead. George Tanner looked at Rider. The sheriff's jaw was set, and he was staring hard at the foreman of the jury.

"What is your verdict?" said Boley.

"Your honor," said the foreman, "we find the defendant not guilty."

Back in his office, Rider tossed Lyons his suitcase. Then he opened a desk drawer and withdrew the pocket pistol he had taken away from Lyons.

"Unload this thing and pack it in your grip," he said, "or I'll arrest you again for carrying a gun in town."

He pitched the pistol at Lyons. Lyons caught it, unloaded it, opened his suitcase, and packed the gun away. Then he closed and relatched his bag. He looked up at Rider with a sneer.

"Lyons," said Rider, "this thing ain't over. Ole Mix was a friend of mine. You ain't getting away with it."

"Even if I was to confess that I had something to do with them killings," said Lyons, "which I ain't, but if I was, you couldn't do nothing to me now. You can't try me twice for the same crime. Ain't that right?"

"You never was tried for killing Jess Halfbreed," said Rider. "I know that you were responsible for the killings."

"Go to hell," said Lyons. He picked up his suitcase and turned to leave the office.

"You'll pay, Lyons," Rider shouted after him.

Lyons had not been gone a minute when Judge Boley walked into Rider's office. He pulled a chair away from the wall and sat down facing Rider.

"There wasn't a thing I could do, Go-Ahead," he said. "I hate this as much as you do. You know that, don't you?"

"I know, Judge," said Rider. "I'm glad you came by. I'm resigning as sheriff. Right now."

Rider unpinned the badge from his vest and dropped it onto the desktop.

"What the hell for?" said Boley. "Man, we can't win them all."

"Mix was a friend, Judge," said Rider, "and so was poor ole Jess. We both know that Lyons is guilty as sin. I ain't letting him get away with what he done. As sheriff, I can't do nothing. That's why I'm resigning. George can keep an eye on things until you all decide what you want to do about a replacement for me. You could do a whole lot worse than George. He's coming along real well."

Boley stood up and paced across the floor.

"I know I can't stop you," he said. "Don't do anything stupid. All right? And be careful."

When Boley left the office, Rider was not far behind. Outside, he found George.

"Where'd he go?" he asked.

"He went to the livery stable," said George.

Rider started walking in that direction.

"Rider," said George. "Let me go with you."

Rider stopped and turned back to face George.

"We already went over that," he said. "I need you to stay here. Otherwise I'd be walking out on this office. I can't do that."

The first thing Rider noticed inside the livery was Lyons's suitcase lying on the floor open and empty. Then he saw Curly walking toward him.

"Curly," he said, "tell me about Lyons. Quick."

"Well, Rider," said Curly, "he just rode out of here."

"He left on horseback?"

"That's right. Bought a horse. That's why he had to empty his suitcase there. He took a slicker out and made a saddle roll."

"Did you see a little pistol?"

"He had it in the suitcase. Loaded it up and put it in his pocket."

"What's he riding?" asked Rider.

"Little spotted mare. You've seen her."

"I know the horse. One more question, Curly. Did you see which way he went when he left out of here?"

"He went out of here riding south," said Curly. "I got a question for you. Where's your badge?"

But Rider didn't bother to answer Curly's question. He was outside in a minute and mounted on the big black from the sheriff's barn. He would settle with the treasurer later for his use of this Cherokee Nation property.

So Lyons had headed south. That was what Rider had figured. Lyons would want the quickest way out of the Cherokee Nation, the quickest way out of the jurisdiction of Go-Ahead Rider. He would be headed for Muskogee, just across the line into the Creek Nation. Muskogee was a new town, a town created overnight by the railroad as it had carved its path through the Indian Nations down into Texas. It was full of crooks and murderers, just the kind of place where Lyons would seek safety. Rider headed for Muskogee.

He was glad he had anticipated all this: a verdict of not guilty and the quick escape of Lyons. He had talked to George before the trial and told him what he would do if things turned out this way. George would go to his house and tell Exie, and George would take care of things at the sheriff's office. Rider had no idea how long this mission would take. He would not—could not—simply murder Lyons. Even though Lyons was himself a murderer, had murdered two of Rider's friends, deserved such a fate, Rider was not a man to do that deed. He didn't know exactly how he would manage it, but somehow he would get Lyons. He would stay close to the man, always be there, await his chance.

Tom Spike Buck was drunk. Earlier in the day he had been less drunk, and he had known better than to go staggering down the main street of Tahlequah. He had been arrested for drunkenness before, and if he were to be caught, arrested, tried, and found guilty again, the punishment would be severe. Earlier he had known that, but he had kept drinking, and he had reached the point where he no longer knew much of anything. He was broke, and he wanted more whiskey, so he was searching for friends from whom he might get a drink or the money to buy one—or several. He had staggered through most of downtown Tahlequah, bumped into several people, followed a wandering path across the street onto the grounds of the capitol building and collapsed on a bench. He did not pass out, but he lacked both the strength and the sense of balance to go further. He stretched out on the bench and watched the treetops above him swirl around in the sky.

George Tanner had gone into the capitol building to talk with Judge Boley. He had wanted Boley's assurance that it was really all right for him to be in charge of the sheriff's office with Rider gone. Boley had given him that assurance. Not only was it all right, Boley had said, there was no other immediate possibility, and besides that, Rider had spoken very highly of George. George left Boley's office with mixed feelings. He was a little afraid of the awesome responsibility Rider had handed over to him. At the same time his ego was puffed up considerably by the thought of Go-Ahead Rider giving him high praise. He left the building, intending to go straight to Rider's house to explain things to Exie. She wouldn't be worried yet. It was not yet time for Rider to be home. But he had to tell her at some point what was going on, and he wanted to get it over with. He had turned to head up the bluff when he saw Tom Spike Buck on the bench. He changed his direction and walked toward the bench.

"Tom," he said.

"Uh?"

Tom Spike Buck raised his head a little and squinted at George.

"Tom, you drunk again?"

"I just had to stop and rest for while, deputy," said Buck. "Is it okay? If it ain't, I'll go on. Just let me rest here few minutes."

George got Buck by one arm and pulled.

"Come on, Tom," he said. "Come along with me."

Buck allowed himself to be dragged up to a sitting position before he began to protest.

"Where we going?" he said.

"We're going to jail, Tom. You're drunk."

Buck stood up and took a wild swing at George. There was not much power behind the swing, and there was even less accuracy, yet the suddenness and unexpectedness of it caught George off guard, and Buck's fist caught George's jaw with a glancing, stinging blow. George drove his right into Buck's stomach, and Buck doubled over in pain. He sank to his knees, both hands gripping at his midsection, groaning. George felt guilty. He could have controlled

Buck with a little manhandling. He knew that. Instead he had hurt him. He had reacted too quickly, and a little bit out of anger. He still had a lot to learn about this job, he thought, and he wished that Rider had been there. God, he thought, I hope he doesn't start to puke.

"Get up, Tom," he said.

Buck rocked slowly back and forth on his knees, still holding his stomach and groaning.

"Come on," said George. "We're going to jail."

"I'm sick."

"Well, you just hold it down until we get to a cell. Then I'll give you a bucket to puke in. Come on."

He reached down and took hold of Buck's arm again. This time Buck allowed himself to be pulled to his feet, and he walked unsteadily alongside George until they reached the jail. George led Buck into the nearest cell and dropped him on the cot. Then he went after the bucket. He set the bucket beside the cot.

"You see that bucket, Tom?" he said. "See it? You get sick, you use that bucket. You hear me? You make a mess on this floor, you're going to clean it up."

He walked out and locked the cell door behind him. Tom Spike Buck seemed to have gone to sleep. George took the keys with him, went on outside, and locked the main door. Then he started toward Rider's house.

He found Exie cleaning in her kitchen. She was always working, he thought. He wondered if the woman ever got a moment's rest other than the time she spent sleeping at night. She was a good woman. She was a good wife to Rider and a good mother to their children. She had been good to George, too. He hoped that she wouldn't be too worried about what Rider was doing, going off in pursuit of Lyons without the protection and authority of his badge. He tried to think of ways to tell her without making her worry. Could he just tell her that Rider would be gone for a while? She would want to know where he had gone and why.

"'*Siyo, Jaji,*" she said, giving his first name the Cherokee pronunciation. She put down her cleaning rag and leaned back against the counter she had been scrubbing. "What brings you home early?"

"I, uh, I've got a message for you from Rider," he said. He felt incredibly nervous all of a sudden. Exie looked at him and waited.

"Uh, he had to go out of town," said George.

"How long?"

"Well, I'm not sure how long he'll be gone. It could be a few days, I guess. I, uh, really don't know for sure."

"They let that man Lyons go?" asked Exie.

Damn, thought George, she's putting it together all by herself.

"Yes," he said, "they did."

"And Rider's going after him, ain't it?"

"Yes. He left his badge here. He resigned."

"I was 'fraid he'd do that. I just knew he would if they let that man go."

She turned her back to George and resumed scrubbing the counter, but she kept scrubbing the same spot. George stood awkwardly, wondering what to do next. He could come up with no words of comfort or assurance. He couldn't just stand there all day, but he couldn't just turn and walk out on her either— not like this.

"It'll be all right," he said feebly. "Rider can take care of himself."

Exie turned on him almost accusingly. The quickness of her movement and the stern expression on her face and the hardness in her voice startled him.

"Go get Beehunter," she said.

George stammered. He felt terribly inadequate to the situation. He should be the one to take control, to reassure her, to protect her while Rider was away. She was taking charge, and there was nothing he could do about it.

"I, uh, I don't know where he lives," he said, "and I can't talk Cherokee. I can't talk to Beehunter."

Exie pulled off her apron and tossed it aside onto the table. She swept past George on her way out the door.

"Come on," she said. "Go with me."

George followed her out the door, and as he did, he smiled to himself in spite of the tense situation. Exie was treating him just as Rider did. And what was more, he was taking it the same way. What else could he do?

Exie, Beehunter, and Beehunter's wife carried on a brief and hurried conversation in Cherokee. George stood by wondering why he was even there. He understood a few words, but only a few. He recognized Rider's name and Lyons's. And he heard Muskogee mentioned, but beyond that he was mostly lost. He felt superfluous. Finally, Exie turned to him.

"Beehunter hasn't got a gun," she said, "or a horse."

"We'll go by the office and issue him a gun," said George. "He can take a horse and saddle from the sheriff's barn."

As soon as he had said that, he wondered about his authority. He could not deputize Beehunter to go out of Tahlequah District, much less clear out of the Cherokee Nation. And if Beehunter was not deputized, did he have the right to, in effect, loan him a horse and gun? Probably not. But these people were the closest thing to family that George had anymore. He loved them like his own family, Rider and Exie and the children. Rider might or might not need help, but Exie definitely needed some sort of solace. Sending Beehunter after Rider would give her that. Right or wrong, George had made his decision.

"Let's go," he said.

Rider knew that Lyons could not be far ahead of him. He figured that even Lyons would know better than to race his mount when he had to travel the distance from Tahlequah to Muskogee. Lyons would be in a hurry, but he would have to go easy or the horse would never make it. Rider, on the other hand, could easily afford to take his time. He knew where Lyons was going, and he was in no hurry to catch up with him somewhere along the road. Unless . . . He had a thought. Up ahead was a place where he could cut across, hurry up just a little, and come out on the road ahead of Lyons. At least he thought he could. If it didn't work, nothing would be lost. If it did, he would have a little more psychological edge on his prey.

He spurred the black and turned off the road. The ground was rocky and uneven underneath a thick and lush growth of tall grass. He had to be careful. He couldn't rush the horse as much as he would have liked. And part of his new path would be through brush and woods. He set a steady pace and let the black have his head. When they reached the woods, he slowed the horse again. There was a narrow, winding path that Rider knew of, and he picked his way through the woods on that.

Finally, they emerged from the woods into another nearly level field. Just across the field was the road. If Rider had calculated right, Lyons would come along the road soon. He rode on down to the road and stopped. He was sitting at a spot where the road just came around a curve and up a steep hill. Lyons would come on him suddenly and all at once. He sat in the saddle and waited.

Back at his office, George unlocked the gun cabinet and pulled out a drawer. He gestured toward the drawer, indicating to Beehunter that he should help himself. Beehunter reached for a Smith and Wesson .44 American. George handed him a box of .44 cartridges. Then Beehunter reached for a Warner single-shot carbine. Well, thought George, who would have taken a Winchester, everyone has his own preference. George handed Beehunter a box of cartridges for the Warner. They left the office and walked to the sheriff's barn, where Beehunter selected a small roan, saddled it, and mounted up. He waved at George, then rode out of town going south.

Lyons was pushing his mount a little too hard. He knew it, and he resolved that he would slow the pace when he got a few more miles away from Tahlequah. He felt good that he had come out of the trial so clean, but he was still afraid of Go-Ahead Rider. The road ahead was steep, and he kicked the horse in the sides to hurry it on up and over the rise.

"Get up," he said. "Come on."

He reached the top of the rise, and there was Rider, sitting in the saddle on his black, off to Lyons's right, not twenty feet away. Lyons yelled out in his surprise and jerked back on the reins. His horse reared up on its hind legs and squealed in surprised fright. Lyons fought it until it stood still and calm again—almost. He looked hard at Rider.

"What are you doing here?" he said. Rider didn't answer. "Damn you, the trial's over. You have to let me go."

"Go on," said Rider. "I ain't stopping you."

"You got no right to bother me anymore," said Lyons.

"I'm just sitting here."

"Damn you to hell," shouted Lyons, and he gave his horse a vicious kick and a lash with the reins. Rider sat still beside the road and watched Lyons race on toward Muskogee. He smiled to himself, and when Lyons had ridden out of sight, he moved out onto the road and followed him at a leisurely pace.

Chapter Twelve

At quitting time that evening, Tom Spike Buck was still asleep. George locked up the office and walked up to Rider's house. Tootie and Buster came running out to meet him. He dropped down on one knee to give the children a hug.

"*Jaji. Jaji,*" they were saying.

With one arm around each child and with their tiny arms reaching around his own neck, George felt tears well up in his eyes. He wondered why. He did love these kids of Rider's, but why the tears today? Because their daddy was off somewhere and could be in danger? Maybe. Because George felt as if he should be with Rider, as if he were somehow betraying these children and their mother by letting Rider face his danger alone? Well, not alone. Beehunter had gone after him. Still, that might be part of it. But there was something else, too. George had been thinking about marriage. He was anticipating his own family. He wasn't really thinking specifically about a family, but he was thinking about Lee Hunt, and if he followed up on his thoughts and if she accepted him, a family would surely follow. Perhaps all of these thoughts together had caused this emotional reaction in George. He pressed the two children tightly to him.

"Hi, kids," he said. "Is your mother in the house?"

"Yes," said Tootie.

"She's cooking," said Buster. "We were waiting for you."

"Let's go in the house," said George.

The meal was on the table just a few minutes after George and the children went in, and they all sat down to eat. Mealtime at Rider's house was usually quiet. They didn't talk. They ate. The talking came after the meal was done. But this night things seemed particularly quiet, unnaturally quiet. Rider's chair was empty, and everyone at the table was very much conscious of that unhappy fact.

When the meal was finished, George tried to help Exie with the dishes. He had never done that before. Normally after a meal George and Rider went out on the dog run and sat and talked and drank coffee, and Rider smoked his pipe. George wasn't sure why he felt obligated to try to help Exie with the dishes on this particular occasion, but it didn't matter. She wouldn't allow it. She told him that she didn't want him in her kitchen. He looked around for other chores to do, things that Rider might have done had he been home. But things were pretty well in order. After all, Rider hadn't been gone one night yet. Finally Exie took pity on George's predicament.

"George," she said, "you're doing enough by being at the office. Rider needs that. Stop worrying about me. Why don't you go on down and visit your girl? Huh? Go on. We're okay here."

George started walking to Lee Hunt's house. Exie had called Lee his girl. He had never put it that way before, and he kind of liked the sound. "My girl," he said out loud. "My girl." He wondered if he would have the nerve to ask Lee to marry him. Was it too early? He knew already that he wanted her, but he didn't know how she would react to such a proposal. He didn't want to spoil what he already had by being too bold. Well, he thought, he would wait and see how the conversation went. If it seemed right, he would ask her—maybe.

He walked past the jail, and everything was dark and quiet. He wondered if Tom Spike Buck had yet come out of his drunken stupor. He walked on. When he came to the street that Lee lived on, he turned to walk up to her house. Then he stopped. There in front of her house, a buggy was parked. She had visitors. Or a visitor. He stood a moment, staring at the buggy, fighting off an impulse to sneak up to the house and try to spy out who was there. Then he turned, dejected, and started walking back, retracing his steps. He didn't want to go back to Rider's house—not so soon. He stopped at the jail and unlocked the front door. Inside the office, he lit the lamp. Then he walked with it down the hall to the cell where he had left Tom Spike Buck. Buck saw the light and slowly raised himself up to a sitting position on the cot.

"Hello, Tom," said George. "How are you feeling?"

"I'm real sick," said Buck.

"You want something to eat?"

"No. I can't eat. I'm too sick."

"How about some coffee?"

"You . . . got anything else?"

"You know better than that, Tom. It's coffee or nothing. You want it?"

Buck's face twisted in a painful grimace, and he rubbed it with both hands.

"Yeah," he said, his voice a whine. "I guess so."

"I'll be back in a few minutes," said George, and he went back to the office to put on the coffee. While he waited for it to boil, he sat behind Rider's desk. His thoughts drifted from Rider to Lee. What was Rider doing? Had he caught up with Lyons? If he had, what then? And what about Beehunter? Where was he? He hoped that Rider could manage to do whatever it was he intended to do without getting himself into trouble. Would Rider simply murder Lyons? George didn't think so, yet he knew that Rider was determined that Lyons would not get away with what he had done, with what they knew he had done even though they had not been able to prove anything. But what about the belief that a man is innocent until he is proven guilty? Did they really know that Lyons was responsible for the deaths of Mix Hail and Jesse Halfbreed? If they couldn't prove it, how could they say they knew it?

He wished that he could discuss this problem with Lee. Lee. Who was at her house? What were they discussing? George wondered if it was a man visiting Lee. Did he have a rival? And what if that man was having the same thoughts about her that George was having? And if so, what if he asked the question first? Would she accept? Then George had another and even more disquieting thought. He wondered if the man at Lee Hunt's house would spend the night there as he had done. If so, would it be on a pallet on the floor?

The coffee should be ready, he thought, consciously working to push the other, less pleasant thoughts from his mind. He got up to check it. It was ready, and he got a cup for himself and one for Tom Spike Buck. He carried the coffee and the lamp down the hall to the cell, handed Buck his cup through the bars, and pulled a three-legged stool up beside the cell to sit on.

"Where'd you buy your booze, Tom?" he said. "We busted Riley's supply all up."

"Oh," said Buck, "there's other places. I don't know where. There's lot of places."

He sipped at the hot coffee and made faces as he swallowed. He looked as if drinking the coffee would make him sick. George was glad he had put the bucket in the cell. He sipped his coffee and watched Buck. He wondered about this man. What had made him this way? Him and others like him. Jesse Halfbreed. George had not known Jesse, not really, but Rider had said that Jesse was a friend of his. There was a tendency to dismiss men like Jesse and

Tom as worthless drunks and forget about them, but George wondered. They were men, after all, he thought.

"So you busted all Riley's stuff?" said Buck.

"That's right."

"You killed him, too, didn't you?"

"Yes," said George, "I did. But not because of the liquor."

"You killed him because he killed Jess and Mix for that Omer, ain't it?"

George was about to take a sip of coffee. He stopped still. He looked over the cup at Tom Spike Buck. His mouth hung open as if it wanted to form words, but no words came. Not for a long and quiet moment. Then George reached down and put his cup on the floor. He stood up and walked to the bars.

"Tom," he said, his voice quiet, "what did you say?"

"I said you killed Riley."

"You said more than that. You said why."

"Oh," said Buck. He took a loud slurp from his coffee cup. "Oh, yeah."

"Why?" said George. "Why did I kill Riley? Tell me again."

"I thought it was 'cause he killed Jess—and Mix."

"For someone else?"

"Yeah. For that Omer Lyons who worked for the railroad."

George took a couple of deep breaths. He felt stunned. He could scarcely believe what he was hearing.

"Wait a minute, Tom," he said. "Wait a minute. I'll be right back."

He rushed back to the office and got the keys he had dropped on Rider's desk. Then he went back to the cell and unlocked the door. He took the lamp and his cup.

"Come on, Tom," he said. "Let's go to the office where we can talk better. Come on."

Buck got to his feet. He was still unsteady.

"You all right?" said George. "You need to bring that bucket?"

God, he hoped that the man didn't puke in the office.

"Naw," said Buck. "I'm all right. I'm just sick is all."

George led Buck into the office and gave him a chair to sit in. Then he sat down behind Rider's desk.

"More coffee?" he said.

"Yeah."

He got up and refilled the cup. Then he resumed his seat, Rider's chair.

"Tom?"

"Yeah?"

"Tom, we arrested Bean Riley on suspicion of murder—the murders of Mix Hail and Jess Halfbreed. We had good evidence against him. If he had stood trial he would have been convicted, and he would have been hanged. We knew that he killed them both. Are you listening to me?"

Buck nodded his head slowly.

"Yeah," he said.

"All right," said George. "We knew he had killed those two men. That's why we arrested him. Then he escaped from jail and we went after him. I killed him because he was about to kill me. He didn't give me any choice. That's the only reason I killed him. Do you understand that?"

"Oh, yeah. Sure," said Buck. Again he nodded his head. George thought that it was an exaggerated nod, and that together with the tone of Buck's voice made George read Buck's answer, "Okay, if that's your story, I won't argue with it."

"Damn it, Tom," George said. "We wanted the trial. We wanted to get more information out of Riley. I didn't want to kill him."

Buck rolled his yellow eyes up and looked at George for the first time. He nodded again.

"Now," said George, "you said that Riley killed Mix Hail and Jess Halfbreed. Did you know he did that?"

"Yeah," said Buck. "I knew."

"You said he did it for Lyons. Did you know that?"

"Yeah."

"This is very important, Tom," said George. "Tell me how you knew."

"Ah," said Tom. "I don't know. I don't remember."

"Tell me, Tom."

"I'm sick. This coffee is making me sick."

George had a quick thought. It was probably illegal and maybe even immoral, but he didn't have Rider to advise him. He was on his own, and he was in charge. The stakes were high.

"What do you need, Tom?" he said. "You need some whiskey? You have any money?"

"No," said Tom, his head hanging.

"I don't have any whiskey. I don't even know where to get it. Not after we broke all of Riley's stuff. But I've got some money, Tom. Here. Take it."

He reached into a pocket and pulled out a few coins. He didn't know just what the price of illegal whiskey was, but he was sure he'd given Buck enough.

"Here," he said. "It's yours."

Tom Spike Buck had a suspicious look on his face, but he held out his hands and took the money. Then he closed his fist tight. He put down the coffee cup. He started to stand up, but George interrupted him.

"You're stuck here in jail, though, Tom," he said, "and I'm the only one who can let you out. Rider's not here. Just me. I'm the only one."

Buck sagged back in the chair. He had money in his hands, but he was a prisoner. He wanted whiskey real bad. His head was hurting. He was sick.

"How did you know, Tom?" said George. "How did you know that Riley killed those men for Lyons? Did Lyons pay him? Tell me. I'm the only one holding you here."

"I worked for Riley," said Buck. "He paid me to shoot at Jess that time. That time you and Rider brought us to jail. He paid me to do that. He said it was a joke. Then I seen Mix. I seen the body in the springhouse with all the whiskey, and Bean caught me in there. But he gave me some whiskey, and he said it was all right because the railroad men were paying him. He got me to help him move Mix out on the road. Then he wanted me to help him kill Jess, but Jess was my friend. He said Lyons would pay a lot of money. I took some of his whiskey and I went off and hid. I didn't want to do it. That's how I know."

George heaved a deep sigh and leaned back in Rider's chair. He sat quietly for a moment, letting this new information soak in. Then he stood up quickly and walked around the desk.

"You can go, Tom," he said. "Go on home. You're free."

"When's my court day?" said Buck.

"No court day. No charges. You haven't even been in jail. Just get on out of here."

Tom Spike Buck stood up slowly. He didn't know whether or not to believe this new deputy. He eased himself toward the door.

"I can go?" he said.

"Yes," said George.

"I don't got to come back to court?"

"Not this time."

Buck turned and hurried out the door. Right or wrong, thought George, I got it. I got what we wanted, what we needed. Damn. I wish I could talk to Rider right now. But he knew he couldn't. He was stuck in Tahlequah, and he really had no idea where Rider would be by this time. Rider had thought that Lyons would head for Muskogee, but the man could have changed directions. There was no telling for sure. He'd just have to wait for Rider to get back and hope for the best. He forced himself to sit down at his own desk and make some notes based on what Tom Spike Buck had told him, then he turned off the lamp, locked the building, and left. He left, but he didn't walk back toward Rider's house. He walked back toward Lee's house. The buggy was gone. He breathed a sigh of relief and turned to go home to Rider's. It was too late to call on Lee. He would see her tomorrow, he hoped. Tomorrow would be a busy day. Or maybe not. Maybe it would be a frustrating day. Maybe he would spend the day sitting around wondering what he could do with this new information. *What would Rider do in this situation? What would Rider do?*

He went to sleep that night with questions tormenting his mind. *Where was Rider? What would Rider do if he were here? What should I do?* Who was at Lee's house tonight? In his fitful sleep, the questions became images that caused him to toss uneasily in his bed. He saw Rider step up behind Omer Lyons and pull out his two big Colts. Saw him point both big guns at Lyons's back and slowly, deliberately pull the triggers. Saw the bullets tear into Lyons's back, and saw Lyons fall forward, screaming as he landed on his face in the dirt. Then he saw a fancy buggy pulled by a fine white horse pull up in front of Lee Hunt's house, and a handsome, well-dressed man get out. The man walked confidently, arrogantly up to her front door and rapped on it with the head of a walking stick. Lee opened the door and threw herself into the man's arms. They kissed passionately. Outside he saw a posse of heavily armed lawmen surround Rider. Then Rider was inside a courtroom, and the judge was shouting, "Guilty. Guilty," and pounding his gavel, and out in the courtroom among the crowd of spectators, he saw Exie and Tootie and Buster, and on the other side of the room Lee and the handsome stranger. And he saw Tom Spike Buck, reeling drunkenly and laughing, and he knew that Buck had got that way on the money he had given him.

In Muskogee, sitting on the back of his black horse in the shadow of some tall trees, Go-Ahead Rider watched Omer Lyons go into James L. Barnes's Pioneer Boarding Car, a hotel made up of five railroad cars parked on a sidetrack. Lyons would get his room and go to sleep. He had lived through a rough day. He was in the Creek Nation, beyond Rider's jurisdiction, and he would feel safe. He would sleep late in the morning.

Rider could afford to get a good night's sleep. He knew he would be up long before Lyons, and he knew where Lyons would be. He rode out of town to the edge of the river, and he made himself a camp. He would spend the night there, and in the morning, he would go back into Muskogee, find himself a place to have breakfast, and then return to the Pioneer Boarding Car and wait for Lyons

Chapter Thirteen

Omer Lyons crawled out of bed in the luxurious Pioneer Boarding Car. He felt pretty good. Things, of course, would have been better had the vote in Tahlequah come out in his favor. He would have gotten more money out of the railroad, and he might even have worked his way into a permanent position with them. But he had been paid reasonably well by the railroad while the Council meeting lasted, and he still had money. Then things had gotten bad, but he had come out of the whole mess slick, and he had removed himself from the reaches of the Cherokee authorities. He was safe. His money would last for a while yet. Before it was gone, he would find something else to do.

He washed his face in the basin of water in the room, and he dressed. He didn't need to shave. Maybe tomorrow. He had just enough Indian blood in him to have inherited a light beard. He dropped the little three-shot pistol into his right-hand coat pocket and left the room. As he stepped down from the train car hotel, he saw Go-Ahead Rider standing to his right, not five feet away from him. Rider was leaning on the side of the car, his arms folded across his chest. The grips of his big Colts were visible beneath his folded arms.

"Morning, Omer," said Rider.

Lyons struggled to regain his composure. He turned to face Rider.

"You're out of your jurisdiction," he said.

Rider unfolded his arms and held them out to his sides.

"Look," he said. "No badge. I quit."

"Then what do you want with me?"

"Nothing, Omer. Why would I want you? I'm just over here for a little change in scenery. That's all."

"Leave me alone," said Lyons, and he hurried away from the car. After he had gone some fifty feet, he stopped, turned, and looked back at the hotel on wheels. Go-Ahead Rider was nowhere to be seen.

George ate breakfast with the Riders, then went directly to find Elwood Lovely. He found Lovely at Al's Eats, having a last cup of coffee following a big breakfast.

"Mr. Lovely," said George.

"Call me Woody," said the marshal. "Everyone else does."

"Mind if I sit with you?"

"Hell, no. Take a load off. You ate yet?"

"Yes," said George. "I have. I could stand a little more coffee, though."

Lovely raised a hand.

Al brought a cup and the pot. He poured George some coffee and refilled Lovely's cup.

"What's on your mind?" said Lovely, after Al had left them.

"Well," said George, "I've got something to tell you. At first I didn't know if I should tell you or not. I'm still not quite sure, but I did get some new information that helped me decide."

Lovely took a sip of coffee and waited for George to continue. The man was already hesitant, he thought. Don't rush him.

"Rider turned in his badge yesterday," George said.

Surprise registered on Lovely's face, but still he kept quiet.

"He went after Lyons. I guess you heard about the results of the trial. Lyons was found not guilty. We just didn't have any real evidence against him. Anyhow, Rider said he knew that Lyons had paid Riley to do the killing for him, and he wasn't about to let him get away with it. So he went after him."

"Where'd they go?" asked Lovely.

"When Lyons left out of here he was headed south. Rider speculated that he was going to Muskogee."

"What are you worried about, George? You afraid that Rider's going to get himself killed?"

"No, sir," said George. "Oh, maybe a little. What I'm really worried about is that Rider might go and commit a murder and get himself in trouble with the law over there. I don't want to see that happen."

"I think Rider's too smart for that," said Lovely, "but it is a danger. It could happen."

"Woody, last night I got evidence that would have convicted Lyons if we'd had it before the trial. It would still convict him, I think, if we had him again."

"You can't try a man twice for the same crime, George. Lyons is free."

"I know," said George, "but we only tried him for the murder of Mix Hail. My new evidence would have convicted him of that, but it would also convict him of the murder of Jess Halfbreed. We didn't charge him with that one."

"George," said Lovely. He stood up, and took a last, long slurp from his cup. "You go see Harm Boley and get a fugitive warrant for Lyons. I can't serve it on him, but it will add a little clout if

I can show it. I carry blank whiskey warrants with me all the time, and I can arrest a man with one of them anywhere I find him. But if you get me that other warrant, I'll use that as justification for bringing him back here to you. I'll meet you in front of the capitol building to get it, and then I'm going to Muskogee."

Most of the day had gone by, and George had discovered that, with the single exception of his early morning conversation with Elwood Lovely, his speculation of the night before that it would be a long and frustrating day had been correct. Soon it would be time to lock the office and go home. That meant going to Rider's house. George felt a little uncomfortable being in Rider's house with his family during his absence. He would go, of course. For one thing he had no other home to go to. He also felt an obligation to Rider and his family. There might be something around the house that needed doing while Rider was gone, something that Exie couldn't handle alone, or something that George could accomplish much more easily than she could. He would go to Rider's house, eat supper, and see if there was any way he could be of help. Then perhaps he would go out again and—do what? Patrol the town? Maybe. He wanted to go visit Lee Hunt, but he still didn't know who her other visitor had been. Well, he would go out and do something until it was late enough to go back and go to bed. He stood up and went to the coffeepot. He knew that he had already had too much coffee. He was beginning to feel just a little light-headed. But it was a boring and trying day. He had just lifted the pot to pour himself another cup when Vernon Starr walked into the office.

"Tanner?" said Starr.

"Yeah?"

"We met once," said Starr. "I'm Vern Starr, Cherokee Nation Treasurer."

"Sure," said George, extending his hand. "I remember."

"Did you know that today is payday?"

"Oh," said George. "I guess I hadn't thought about it. No one said anything. I haven't had one yet."

"That's what I thought when it got to be so late in the day and you hadn't showed up in my office. I brought your money and a receipt for you to sign showing that I gave it to you. The normal procedure is for you to stop by the office on payday, but since Rider's gone, I figured I could come over here this time and let you know."

"Thanks," said George. "I appreciate that. I guess I'd have just gone on and never known the difference."

"You'd have thought about it before much longer, I expect. If you'll just sign this," said Starr, handing George a slip of paper, "I'll give you your money and be on my way."

George took the receipt to his desk and signed it, then handed it back to Starr. The treasurer then carefully counted out a small stack of coins onto the desktop.

"There you go," he said. "Don't spend it all in one place."

"Well," said George, "I might."

The money lifted his spirits some. It surprised him. He hadn't, he thought, been overly conscious of his dwindling assets. He had been too busy with other concerns. But looking at the stack of coins on his desk did make him feel better. He picked up the money and felt its weight in his palm. Then he dropped it into a pocket, looked around the office, picked up the keys, and left. It was still a little early, but nothing was happening. No one was in jail. His duties might as well take him around the town as keep him sitting in the office. So he walked downtown. He stopped in at Jameson's Boot and Shoe Store and bought himself a pair of new, high-topped, black boots. He pulled them on and stuffed his trouser legs down inside them.

"If you'll wrap up my old shoes," he said, "I'll just wear these."

From there he went to the newest mercantile store in Tahlequah, just down the street from Jameson's, where he tried on several hats. Finally satisfied with his appearance under the wide, flat brim of a black Plainsman with a red and white woven hatband, he paid for the hat and left. He felt good with his new hat and boots and some money still left in his pockets. He tried to think of what else he needed now that he had been paid. The only thing he could come up with was a place to live, a place of his own, but he wouldn't do anything about that yet, not until Rider had returned. He strolled casually down the sidewalk, his package under his left arm. He walked to the end of the street, turned, and walked back as far as the mercantile. He went back in.

"Do you have a nice scarf for a lady?" he asked.

"Kerchief?"

"Yeah. Whatever you call it. What do you have?"

"Right this way, sir."

The clerk led George to a counter that was stacked with scarves. He held some up for George to see. George picked up a few and looked at them and felt them. The clerk moved over to another counter.

"We have some very nice shawls," he said.

"Uh, shawls?" said George turning to follow the clerk.

"For around the shoulders."

"Yeah."

"Like this for instance," said the clerk, holding up a large square piece of material and folding it into a triangle. It was blue with yellow flowers printed all over and a lace border. The clerk flung it around his own shoulders to let George see how it would look when worn.

"That will do," said George. "That's nice."

"I have some others here."

"No. I'll take that one."

He paid for his latest purchase and left the store, then he headed for Rider's house. When he got to the top of the hill, the kids ran to meet him as usual, and he gave them his usual hug. They went inside and had their supper. George didn't feel quite as uneasy as he had the day before. All three Riders complimented George on his new hat and boots, and they made some other small talk when they were finished eating.

"Exie," said George, "is there anything I can do for you around the house?"

"Everything's done, George," she said.

"I bought something today for Miss Hunt," said George. "I want to show it to you."

He picked up his package and took out the shawl, holding it up for Exie to see.

"Will she like it, do you think?"

"Oh, yes," said Exie. "Sure she will. It's real pretty."

"Good. Thanks. Well, if you don't have anything for me to do around here, I think I'll go by and see if Lee—if Miss Hunt is home."

He took both packages and crossed the dog run into the other cabin, the one in which he was staying. He tossed the old shoes into a corner and went to rummage among his books. He found his copy of the fifth edition of Whitman's *Leaves of Grass*, published in 1871. It was practically brand new and absolutely the latest thing that he had. She might possibly have an earlier edition. He had no way of knowing, but certainly she wouldn't have this. It couldn't have reached the Cherokee Nation yet. He took out the shawl and wrapped it around the book, then put the wrapped book back into the paper package the shawl had come in. Then he walked to her house.

No buggy was parked in front. George breathed a sigh of relief, walked up to the door, and knocked. From inside, Lee opened the door a crack so that she could peek out and see who was there. Then she flung it wide open and stepped back out of the way.

"George," she said, "come in."

George stepped in and closed the door.

"I'm glad you're home," he said. "I wanted to see you. And I'm glad that you're not occupied. I came by yesterday, but you had company, so I went on."

"Oh," said Lee, "my superintendent was here with his wife. We had a—nice visit."

George tried hard to take that welcome news casually, but he was greatly relieved to find out that the buggy he had seen did not belong to some rival suitor. He held the package out toward Lee.

"I brought you something," he said.

"A present?"

She took the package and reached in, pulling out the shawl-wrapped book. The paper was dropped to the floor and ignored. Carefully she unwrapped the book.

"George," she said, "I don't know what to look at first. Here. You hold this."

She handed him the book and draped the shawl around her shoulders. She stepped over to a mirror on the wall to get a look. She turned one way and then another. George watched, smiling. She's awfully lovely, he thought. He felt good. It had been money well spent.

"It's beautiful, George," she said. "Thank you. Now, let me see the rest."

She took the book back from George and studied its cover.

"*Leaves of Grass*. Walt Whitman," she said. "I've heard of Mr. Whitman, of course, but I've never read any of his work."

"This is the latest edition," said George. "The fifth. Of all the books I brought back from the East, this is the newest. Mr. Whitman was not well received by the critics at first, but they are beginning to praise him. I think he was probably ahead of his time. As a poet. He's a kind of—innovator, I suppose."

"I look forward to becoming acquainted with him. Thank you again. Can I get you some coffee?"

"Well, yes," said George. "I'll have some."

"Sit down. I'll just be a minute."

George sat in the rocker, and soon Lee brought in coffee and cookies.

"Have you been busy?" she asked.

"Well, yeah. Kind of. Rider's out of town, and I guess I'm more or less in charge."

"And you were paid today," said Lee.

"Yeah," said George. "How did you know?"

"Your new hat and new boots and my shawl."

George ate a cookie in one bite, and then he washed it down with a big swallow of coffee.

"I thought you had a beau," he said.

"What?"

"Well, I mean, I was afraid that you might. When I saw that buggy here last night, I was afraid it might be some other man calling on you. I'm glad I was wrong."

Lee smiled and stared at George for a long, silent moment.

"George," she said, "I like you."

It wasn't hard for Omer Lyons to find a man in Muskogee from whom to buy whiskey, and as he was paying the man, he whispered a harsh and desperate question. The man pointed to two other men standing not far away. Lyons nodded and walked over to the two strangers.

"Buy you a drink?" he said.

The two eyed him suspiciously and looked at each other, and then the smaller of the two said, "Sure."

"Where can we go that's safe?" said Lyons.

"Follow me," said the same man who had spoken before.

Lyons followed the two toughs. They led him to a dirty canvas tent pitched not far from the railroad tracks, and they crawled inside. Apparently they lived in there. The filth and the stench almost overwhelmed Lyons, but he was desperate. He pulled out the bottle he had just purchased and uncorked it. He took a swig, and then he handed it to the smaller of the two men. The whiskey felt good to Lyons. It was the first he had tasted since before Bean Riley's stock had been destroyed.

"My name's Lyons," he said.

"Branham," said the small man.

Lyons looked at the other, who had just finished his first pull at the bottle. The man wiped his mouth with his sleeve and handed the bottle back to Lyons.

"Crider," he said.

Lyons wanted to wipe off the mouth of the bottle before touching it back to his own lips, but he was afraid he might offend the two ruffians he had picked up. He steeled himself and took another swig, then handed the bottle back to Branham.

"There's a man following me," he said. "I want him off my trail. Someone said you might help."

Branham handed the bottle to Crider and stared at Lyons without responding. God, thought Lyons, these two would slice their own mothers' throats for a dollar. He reached into a pocket and pulled out some money. He held it out to Branham. Branham took the money and looked at it. Still, he did not speak. Crider handed the bottle back to Lyons. Lyons took another drink.

"If you get him off my back," he said, "I'll give you the same amount again."

He handed the bottle to Branham. Branham took a long drink and passed the bottle on to Crider.

"What's his name?" he asked.

"His name is Go-Ahead Rider."

"Injun?"

"Yes."

"Where do we find him?"

"I don't know where he's staying," said Lyons, "but I'm staying at the Pioneer Boarding Car. He hangs around there at night and again in the morning, just watching me. You can find him there. But don't do anything there. Follow him to wherever he stays and do it there. Away from me. When it's done, you can find me at the Pioneer, and I'll give you the rest of your money."

Chapter Fourteen

Rider waited again that night beside the converted railroad car in which Omer Lyons would sleep. Branham and Crider saw him there. They had arrived by plan ahead of Lyons. They took up a position about thirty yards from the car, leaning against a tree. They tried to appear casual. Branham sat on the ground and leaned back against the tree trunk. He was facing away from the hotel car and Rider, but in such a manner that he could still watch Rider out of the corner of his eye. Crider stood leaning back on the tree trunk around the other side. He could not see Rider, nor Rider him. Their trick did not work, though. Rider noticed the two ruffians. Rider filled and lit his pipe. Crider pulled out a plug of chewing tobacco and a penknife. He cut himself off a chew and offered some to Branham.

"Naw," said Branham. "That's a filthy habit."

He took out a sack of Bull Durham and a paper and rolled himself a cigarette. Digging a wooden match out of his pocket, he struck it and lit the smoke.

"That's our man over there by the car," he said. "You see him?"

"I can't see him now," said Crider, "but I seen him when we first come up. You sure that's him?"

"He fits the description ole Lyons give us. Well, don't he?"

"This town's full of goddamn redskins. They all look the same to me. How do I know?"

"Well, we'll know as soon as Lyons shows up," said Branham. He took a pull on his cigarette and exhaled loudly. Crider spat out a thick stream of dark brown liquid. A bit of it dribbled down his chin.

"He's a-coming now," he said.

"Sidle on around here a ways," said Branham, "and help me keep a watch. But don't let that Injun see that we're a-watching him."

"We going to kill him now?"

"Not unless he jumps Lyons."

Lyons approached the hotel by a path that led him to within four yards of the tree sheltering Branham and Crider. As he passed the tree, he spoke in a low voice.

"That's him," he said.

"I told you," said Branham to his partner.

"So you were right," said Crider. "I figured it was him. I just said that I didn't know. I can't tell one from the other. Now we know for sure. That's all."

Lyons approached the car. Rider did not move. He puffed his pipe. Lyons made out as if he didn't even notice Rider standing there until he had climbed the steps and was about to go through the door of the car. Then he turned to face Rider.

"You trying to smoke me?" he said. "I know all about that Indian medicine. You think that smoke of yours will do something to me, don't you? Well, I don't believe in that nonsense. It's savage, heathen superstition, that's all it is. Besides, I got some medicine of my own."

"Yeah," said Rider, "I see them. Over there by that big cottonwood. Right?"

"I don't know what the hell you're talking about," said Lyons, and he went quickly inside the car, shutting the door after himself. Rider kept puffing his pipe until it went out. Then he knocked out the ashes and pocketed the pipe.

"He going to stay there all damn night?" asked Crider.

"Just shut up and be patient," said Branham.

Rider walked to the hitchrail where he had left the big black horse. He unwrapped the reins from the rail, climbed into the saddle, and turned the horse around. He looked directly at Branham and Crider, smiled, and then touched the brim of his hat. Crider looked away quickly. Branham, more cool, reached up slowly and touched the floppy brim of his old slouch hat. The surly expression on his face never changed. Rider headed north toward his riverside camp. They'll be along in a minute, he thought. It's Lyons's style.

"Let's go," said Crider.

"Hold on," said Branham. "Don't be in such a hurry. You'll just get us killed. He thinks he's got us figured out. He's expecting us to follow him. We done lost our surprise, so we got to go slow and easy."

Crider spat.

"All right," said Branham. "Let's go."

Branham stood up and led the way to a spot another twenty yards distant, where two ragged-looking ponies waited. They mounted the ponies, and Branham again led the way.

"You've let him get a head start of us," said Crider. "How do we know where he's gone?"

"He headed down that trail to the river," said Branham. "Likely he's got a camp down there. We'll find him."

Crider was anxious, nervous. He wanted to race ahead and catch

Rider and blast him out of the saddle. Branham held him back. He rode ahead and he rode slow and easy.

"Damn it," said Crider. "We're going to lose him."

"Ain't no place he can turn off this road," said Branham. "I know this road. He's straight up there ahead of us. We keep on easy like this, by the time we get there, he'll be done bedded down. Then we slip up on him real easy-like, and he just won't never wake up again. That's all. You get it?"

"All right. All right," said Crider. "But I don't like it."

Rider knew that the two men he had seen back at the Pioneer Boarding Car would follow him to his camp. He knew that they had tried to appear to be just lounging about, to be a couple of vagrants, to be not interested in him, and, therefore, he knew, or at least he felt reasonably certain, that they would not follow him too closely. If they were at all familiar with the area, they would realize at once that he was headed for the river, and they would quickly assume that he had a camp there or was planning to make one. They would lay back and plan to sneak up on him at his campsite, preferably after he had gone to sleep for the night. Well, he thought, he would accommodate them. He would hurry up just a bit in order to get back to his campsite in time to make a few preparations to receive his uninvited guests in the manner they deserved. He would be ready for them.

Branham called an unexpected halt and got down out of his saddle. Crider hauled back on his reins but stayed mounted.

"What the hell you doing now?" he said. "Let's go get it over with."

"I think we're too close," said Branham. "I let your faunching get to me, and we started out too soon. We'll wait here long enough for me to smoke a cigarette and for him to get his camp set up and crawl under a blanket. Then we'll move out again. I want him bedded down before we sneak up on him."

"I still think we ought to just ride up behind him and blast him out of the saddle. That's what I think," said the nervous Crider.

"And what's he going to do when he hears two horses racing up behind him? Just sit there and wait for us to do as we damn please? Out here like this at night, he'd hear us coming before we got close enough to put a bullet in his back. You can hear farther at night. Didn't you know that?"

"Aw," said Crider, "that's bullshit. Distance don't change. Your ears don't change."

"It's true. You *can* hear farther at night. Shut up and listen."

The two were silent for a moment as Branham rolled himself a cigarette.

"I don't hear nothing," said Crider. "Near or far. Nothing."

"Then just humor me," said Branham, striking a match. He inhaled to light the cigarette. "I don't want to argue with you."

Branham sucked deeply on his smoke, and Crider reluctantly dismounted. He let his reins drop and trail on the ground, and he sat down beside his partner, leaning back against the same tree trunk.

"I just want to get it over with," he said. "That's all."

"It'll be over soon enough," said Branham. "I just want to be sure that it gets over with the way we want it to. You get in too big a hurry, you apt to just get yourself killed. That old Palmer you're carrying is a single-shot."

"One shot's all I need," said Crider with a sneer.

"I damn hope so." said Branham, "but if you miss, then all we got is pistols, and with them, we got to be in damn close to be sure."

"All right. All right. Hell," said Crider. "Well, have we waited long enough now?"

Branham took a last long drag off his cigarette, tossed the butt away, and heaved himself to his feet.

"Let's go," he said.

They rode slowly and cautiously, Branham again in the lead. Every few yards, Branham would stop, sit and listen, then move ahead again. Soon he halted and dismounted again. This time he tied his horse to a low branch at the edge of the trail.

"Not again," said Crider.

"Shh. Shut up," whispered Branham. "The river's just ahead. We go on from here afoot."

Crider climbed down and tied his mount, then pulled the Palmer single-shot bolt-action carbine out of its scabbard and thumbed back the outside hammer. Both men moved forward on the trail at a low crouch. Branham held in his left hand a Plant .42 revolver. Crider, in addition to his carbine, had a Smith and Wesson .32 revolver in his belt. They took cautious steps, moving slowly and planting each foot carefully to make as little noise as possible. Soon they saw the small camp fire. They paused instinctively, and then at Branham's signal, moved ahead again. Once they were a little closer they could see the outline of the man. He was not quite sitting up, but he wasn't really lying down either. Obviously, if Branham had wanted to catch the man asleep, they hadn't waited long enough. The man's back was toward them. He seemed to be on his back but propped up on his elbows. His head was up and his hat was on his head. Branham motioned Crider to move in a little closer. With only one rifle shot to count on, Branham wanted to get within easy pistol range before giving away their presence. When he felt comfortable with the distance, he raised his Plant .42 at arm's length, took careful aim, and shouted and fired at once.

"Now."

The Plant spat flame, and Crider's carbine cracked. Crider dropped the carbine and hauled out his .32 revolver. The two men walked closer with every shot, and every shot hit its mark. They could tell. But there was something unnatural about the target. Branham stopped. He held up a hand to stop Crider as well. He stared hard at the target up ahead by the small camp fire, but he couldn't see it clearly enough. He was afraid to move in closer, not without knowing. His revolver was empty.

"Crider," he whispered harshly. "Your gun empty?"

"Yeah. I hit him every shot, too."

"Shut up and reload."

Crider didn't understand, but the fear and desperation he detected in Branham's voice transferred quickly to his own heart, and he reached into his coat pocket for bullets. Branham was doing the same.

"Just hold still," said Rider from somewhere in the dark. "You start to reload, I'll kill you."

Branham quickly summed up the situation. The man could probably drop them both easily before they could either reload or dive for cover. If his intention was to kill them, he would have done so without calling out to them. He obviously would take them in to the law, if they let him. Probably he would march them back to their horses, have them mount up, and then follow them back to town. If so, there was yet a chance. Branham's 10-gauge Parker shotgun, its barrels sawed off to a mere foot in length, was hanging by a leather thong from the horn of his saddle. He had left it there, thinking that it would be of no use in this ambush. It was loaded.

"All right, mister," he said. "All right. Don't kill us."

"Drop your guns then," said Rider.

Branham dropped his pistol to the ground.

"Do like he says, Crider," he said.

"But, but I—"

"Just do it. Now."

Crider dropped his gun. Then their captor emerged from some thicket off to their left. He walked over to the fire, and they saw him. He held a big Colt in his right hand pointed just about between the two of them, ready to swing in either direction. With his left hand, he reached down for the hat. He put it on his head. Then he pulled a blanket from the target Branham and Crider had riddled with bullets. Beneath it was a pile of fire logs. The man tossed the blanket to one side, then walked away from the fire to where his black horse stood waiting, still saddled. Branham cursed himself silently. He should have noticed the saddled animal. No one would settle down for the night without having unsaddled his horse. The man swung up into the saddle and rode up close to Branham and Crider.

"Your horses are down the road a ways, I guess," he said.

"That's right," said Branham.

"Turn around and start walking," said Rider. "Stay in the middle of the road. Make a sudden move of any kind and I'll kill you. It's a promise."

Branham started walking, and Crider followed. Soon they were back where they had tied their horses.

"Okay," said Rider. "Mount up, slow and easy."

As Crider reached for the reins of his horse to untie it, Branham reached over the saddle for his shotgun. Rider saw the movement just in time. As the shotgun swung into play, Rider threw himself off the black on the side away from Branham. The shotgun blast passed over the saddle just about chest-high. Rider's horse screamed and bolted. Crider ran into the woods, and Branham took a dive for the bushes just as Rider fired a shot in his direction. Then Rider ran off the road for cover. That shotgun had another load. Rider was in the trees on the same side of the road as the other would-be assassin, but he was fairly sure that the man was unarmed. The one to worry about was the one on the other side of the road with the shotgun, and that gun would be useless at much distance. He crouched there in the darkness considering his next move. His horse was out of sight, having run back toward Musko-gee. The other two horses were still tied where they had been all along.

Crider had scampered pretty far into the woods, but he wasn't sure how far. It was dark, and he wasn't a good judge of distance anyhow. He just knew that after he had taken that dive, he had crawled on his hands and knees as fast as he could, and he hadn't stopped until he had run out of breath. His hands and his knees were cut from the crawling, and his face had been lacerated by the brush he had raced through. When he finally stopped moving, he tried to be still and listen. He wondered if it was true that you can hear things at night from farther away than in the daytime. He tried, but he couldn't hear anything but his own heavy breathing.

Maybe that Indian could hear it, too. Slowly he regained control of his breath, and he decided that he had to do something. He couldn't stay in the woods on his hands and knees all night long. He could turn over and sit or stretch out on his back. He could stay like that for a long time, except he was afraid that a snake or a spider might come along and crawl up on his face. Besides all that, he wanted the money that Lyons had promised if he killed the Indian. Slowly he raised himself up on his knees. He waited to see if there would be any reaction to his movement. There was none. He stood up slowly. Still there was nothing. He looked to his left. He couldn't see much for the darkness and the thickness of the woods, but he knew that the river was that way.

If the river was that way, so was the Indian's camp, and so were his guns. If the Indian was busy with Branham, perhaps he could sneak through the woods and get back down there where his guns were just waiting for him. He could reload, sneak up on the Indian's blind side, and kill him. Then Branham wouldn't think he was so damn smart. He started to move through the woods toward the river.

Branham had another shell in the sawed-off shotgun, but he didn't know where his prey had gone. He had seen the man dive off his horse just as he had fired the shotgun, but then the man had taken a shot at him, and Branham himself had headed for cover. The man could be on either side of the road. He wasn't out in the road, not as far as Branham could see. He wished he had his pistol. He would have to get pretty close to use the shotgun. He decided to sit and watch and wait. The man with the most patience, he thought, was the man who would come out alive.

Rider knew just about where Branham had disappeared into the thicket, and he figured the man hadn't moved since his initial plunge into cover. He had kept still and listened for any noise that would be a sign of movement, and he hadn't heard any. Branham had dived into his hole and stayed put. He was sure of that. The other man, the man behind him somewhere in the woods, was unarmed.

They were playing a waiting game, and he guessed that he could play that as well as anyone. But he wasn't sure that was the best strategy. He heard a slight rustling back behind him. It was some distance away, and he figured that the unarmed man was trying to sneak away to safety. He listened. The movement was in the direction of the river, of the river and the camp—and the guns. He had left the guns of those two lying in the road. That was a mistake he should not have made. Now if he continued this waiting game, he could wind up dealing with two armed men out in the dark woods—one on either side. He made a quick decision. He burst out into the road from his hiding place and ran across the road at an angle going toward the river. The angle was calculated to extend the distance between himself and the shotgun. When he was about in the middle of the road, he turned and fired a shot into the woods, aiming in general at the spot where he thought the man was hiding.

Branham came out of the woods and aimed the shotgun. Just as he pulled the trigger, Rider made a dive for the far side of the road. He felt a few pellets bounce off his boots harmlessly, and he rolled and fired three shots back at Branham. The first one struck Branham just under the mouth, shattering his chin and tearing through his throat to exit at the back of his neck. The next two missed their mark as Branham sank to his knees, then fell over on his right side. Rider didn't bother to check on him. The man was probably dead. If not, he was certainly badly hurt and he had fired his last shot. Rider turned and ran back toward his camp.

Crider was fumbling with his Smith and Wesson. He was down on his knees in the road, and he had dropped the first two bullets into the dirt. He had gotten two into the chambers and was fumbling with a third when he heard the footsteps of the running man coming toward him. He looked up and saw the form getting closer. He snapped the gun back into firing position and lifted it up. Before he could thumb back the hammer, he felt the dull thud of a bullet in his chest. Then he heard the blast, and then he heard no more.

Chapter Fifteen

Both men were dead. Rider was sorry for that, but they really hadn't given him much choice. On reflection he realized that the one with the shotgun had probably been unarmed when he killed him. He had fired both barrels. Rider had answered the second shot on reflex. Although, of course, he had no way of knowing whether or not the man had reloaded by the time he had fired the second shot, Rider regretted his quick return fire. He walked back to where the first body lay and found the shotgun. Picking it up, he broke it open. One spent shell and one loaded one flew out backward and landed in the dirt behind Rider. So much for the regret, he thought. He checked the man's coat pockets and found several 10-gauge shotgun shells and a handful of .42 caliber bullets. Well, he had better catch his horse. That done, he would load up these two bodies on their own mounts and take them into Muskogee. He wished that he had proof that the men had been hired by Lyons, but he quickly dismissed that thought. Wishing about what was already done was useless. He would just have to keep dogging Lyons's trail until the job was done—one way or another.

It was early morning when Elwood Lovely approached the outskirts of Muskogee. Muskogee was a new town, a railroad town, and it was a lawless, unruly town. Oh, there were a few good citizens in Muskogee, legitimate businessmen with families to raise and an eye to the future, but the majority of the town's population was transient, made up of typical railroad terminus town types: gamblers, sellers of illegal liquor, petty thieves, thugs, and prostitutes. Because of that the federal court at Fort Smith, Arkansas, had established a deputy marshal's office in Muskogee. That would be Lovely's first stop. He would stop in on Deputy Marshal Orrin Mulford and tell him why he had come to Muskogee. Perhaps he and Mulford together could locate Rider and give him the news regarding Lyons, tell him that after all they did have some evidence against Lyons and they could arrest the man on new murder charges. Well, Lovely wasn't sure that he had the authority to arrest a Cherokee citizen for the murder of another Cherokee citizen. That crime came under the jurisdiction of the Cherokee Nation. But Lovely was carrying blank whiskey warrants. He could arrest Lyons for trafficking in illegal liquor in the Indian Territory. That was very much within his jurisdiction. Once Lyons was in his custody, he could transfer the man back to the Cherokee Nation, where the Cherokees could arrest him for the murder of Jesse Halfbreed. And, of course, Lovely would be only too happy to turn his prisoner over to the Cherokees on the more serious charge. The only problems were to find Rider to tell him all this, and then to find Lyons. In Muskogee that could take some time.

Lyons had waited all night in his train car hotel room for the return of his hired killers. Damn it, he thought. Could Rider have gotten them? What did he have to do to get that damn full-blood off his trail? Bean Riley was dead, so there were no witnesses who could be used against him. He had even stood trial and been declared not guilty. He was out of the Cherokee Nation, beyond its jurisdictional reach, yet that son of a bitch Rider had followed him, was hounding him. It wasn't right. He would have to get away, farther away. First he would get across the border into Arkansas, then perhaps Louisiana. New Orleans would be a good place to disappear.

But what if Rider caught up to him first? He felt the three-shot Marston .32 in his pocket. If he was going to have to defend himself against Rider, he'd need better hardware than that. He walked out of the train car and stood for a moment on the top step.

He looked the area over, half expecting to see Rider there, but he was nowhere in sight. Neither did he see anything of the two ruffians he had hired. It was puzzling. If Rider had killed those two, why wasn't he there to hound Lyons as usual? If the would-be killers had done their job, why weren't they around to collect? It didn't make any sense to Lyons, and that made him even more nervous. He hurried away from the hotel toward the business district of Muskogee. He would purchase another gun and then catch the first stagecoach out of town headed east. He hurried along the street, looking back over his shoulder frequently. It was not a particularly hot day, but Lyons was conscious that he was perspiring. He looked across the street, and up ahead, not too far from where he stood, he saw a drugstore. Beneath the sign that said DRUGS was another, this one crudely lettered and tacked onto the siding like an afterthought:

4 SALE
SMITH AND WESTERN
ROOSIAN SIX-SHOOTERS
BEST PRICE ANYWHERE

Lyons hurried over to the drugstore.

"It's got a standard eight-inch barrel," said the clerk, "and it uses what they call a .44 Roosian cartridge. It's a centerfire cartridge." He pulled out a box of the .44 Russians to show Lyons.

"It's got a longer case and a heavier bullet than the Americans. They tell me this slick little son of a bitch was designed by Smith and Western special for the Grand Duke. That's why they call it a Roosian."

"I'll take it," said Lyons. "And a box of shells."

"It's too big for a pocket pistol," said the clerk. "You'll need a holster for it. I got this here slim jim. Specially made for the Roosian, and it's got six bullet loops right on the holster. See. For six extra cartridges. Keep them handy-like."

Lyons walked out of the drugstore with his new Smith and Wesson Russian .44 hanging down his right thigh. Six .44 Russian cartridges were loaded in the pistol and six extra were tucked in the bullet loops on the outside of the slim jim holster. He felt conspicuous. He wasn't used to walking around openly armed. He still had the three-shot Marston in his coat pocket. He felt conspicuous, but somehow he felt safer, more protected. The Russian pistol hanging at his side was heavy, and although he was deeply afraid of Go-Ahead Rider, a part of him was anxious to pull out the big gun and fire it, fire it at the back of Rider, the back, just between the shoulder blades. He tried to imagine what it would look like, the impact of the Russian bullet between Rider's shoulder blades, the way Rider's arms would flail uselessly out to his sides, the manner in which the body would pitch forward and smash, face first, into the hard, rocky ground. He was sweating even harder than before. He walked toward the stagecoach station. Then he hesitated. The stage would take him into Arkansas. What about the railroad? The railroad could take him clear down to Texas. Texas seemed infinitely farther away and boundlessly safe. How could anyone ever find anyone else in Texas? He changed his course for the railroad depot.

Lovely rode up to the deputy marshal's office. He stopped at the hitchrail in front but did not immediately dismount. There were three horses already tied there. One was a big black that had a familiar look about it. The other two were scruffy cow ponies, noticeable only for their scruffiness and for their current burdens. Each pony carried the body of a dead man thrown across its saddle and tied down. The men had obviously been shot. A few people were standing around, looking at the bodies and talking idly about them. Passersby gave them cursory glances and kept on going. The sight of gunshot bodies was not unusual in Muskogee. Lovely swung down out of the saddle, wrapped the reins around the hitch-rail, and went inside. Orrin Mulford sat behind a desk. Go-Ahead Rider was in a straight-back chair across the desk from Mulford.

"Woody," said Mulford. "What brings you to Muskogee?"

"Well," said Lovely, "I actually come over here to get your help. I wanted you to help me locate someone."

"All right," said Mulford. "I'll do what I can. Who you looking for?"

Lovely smiled a halfsmile and pointed a finger at Rider.

"That man right there," he said. "How you doing, Rider?"

"Well," said Rider, "I'm alive. Why you looking for me?"

"You first," said Lovely. "Y'all tell me what's happened here, and then I'll tell my tale. You responsible for them two cadavers out there?"

"I brought them in," said Rider, "and I shot them. I ain't sure that makes me responsible for them, though."

"You two seem to know each other pretty well," said Mulford.

"Rider's the district sheriff over at Tahlequah," said Lovely.

Mulford turned an irritated expression on Rider.

"You didn't tell me that," he said.

"I ain't no more," said Rider. "I knew that I'd be leaving my jurisdiction when I come over this way, so I resigned before I left. Like I told Mr. Mulford here, I was camped out on the river when these two tried to jump me. They shot first. I shot better. That's all."

"Well," said Lovely, going after a chair, "that ain't quite all, now is it? You come over here after Omer Lyons, didn't you?"

Rider looked at the floor. He didn't want to answer that question, had not said anything to Mulford about his mission. He was out to kill a man, a man who had escaped justice. Still it did not seem advisable to confide that information to federal lawmen. Lovely looked from Rider to Mulford.

"Orrin," he said, "first off I want to tell you that Go-Ahead Rider is a good lawman. He's a good man. This fellow Lyons that he's after, he paid a man over in Tahlequah to murder two men, both of them Cherokee citizens. Rider got the man who did the actual killing, but the bastard was killed in an escape attempt. All the evidence against Lyons was circumstantial. They arrested him anyhow and had a trial. Tried him for the one murder. He was let off. Right after the trial, Lyons came over here, to get out of Rider's jurisdiction, I'm sure. Rider here took off his badge and followed him."

He paused for a moment to allow all that to soak into Mulford's head, then he turned back toward Rider.

"I expect that them two you shot was hired by Lyons, too. Don't you reckon that's why they jumped you? That's his style. Hire someone else to do his killing."

Rider's secret was out. There was no sense in trying to hide it any longer from Deputy Mulford.

"Yeah," he said. "That's how I figured it."

"Even if everything Woody said is true," said Mulford, "if you got no proof, you got no right to go gunning for a man."

"I ain't pulled a gun on Lyons," said Rider. "All I've done is just keep an eye on him."

"I get it," Mulford said, leaning back in his chair. "You keep that up long enough, you figure he'll haul down on you. Then you can blow him away and claim self-defense. Is that it?"

"I don't know," said Rider. "All I aim to do is to just dog his trail and see what happens. Them two men he had killed, that was not only in my jurisdiction. They were both friends of mine. I just want to see him get what's coming to him. That's all. I don't care if I do it or someone else does it. I just want to know that it got done."

"Hold it, you two," said Lovely, standing up and pacing away from the desk. He turned and faced the other two men from across the room and continued. "It's my turn now. We have evidence that Lyons bought whiskey from Bean Riley in Tahlequah. I can arrest him on a whiskey warrant. Now I don't really want him for that. If I took him to Fort Smith on that charge and he was found guilty, all he'd have to do is pay a fine. He'd pay it and go on his way. But I could start to take him to Fort Smith by way of Tahlequah, and then Rider here could arrest him on a murder charge."

"I resigned," said Rider. "Remember? I can't arrest nobody. Besides, we done tried him for murder."

"You tried him for the murder of Mix Hail but not for the murder of Jess Halfbreed. You can arrest him—excuse me—George Tanner can arrest him for the murder of Jess Halfbreed. Now hold on. I ain't done yet. George arrested Tom Spike Buck for drunk. Got him in jail and got him to talking. Spike Buck fingered Lyons as the man who paid Riley to do the killings. Young Tanner's got it all wrote down."

Rider stood up from his chair.

"George did that?" he said. "Well, he's coming right along, ain't he? Let's go get Lyons."

Lovely turned back to Mulford.

"Everything all right with you?" he said.

"Yeah. I'll write up them two outside as self-defense based on what Rider here told me and the bullet holes in his hat and you as a character witness for him. Not to mention all that other stuff you just told me. Yeah. Everything's all right with me. Let's go get that bastard Lyons."

George closed up the sheriff's office early and hurried up the hill to Rider's house. He wanted to catch Exie before she started preparing the evening meal. He found her at work sewing. This woman's always working, he thought. She doesn't ever quit. Exie looked up from her work when George stepped into the room.

"You're home early, George," she said. "Everything okay?"

"Oh, yeah," he said. "Everything's fine."

It was nice, he thought, that she referred to the Rider place as his home. He did feel at home with the Riders. He couldn't imagine any better people anywhere in the world, and that was part of the reason he had hurried up to the house early.

"Exie," he said, "don't fix supper tonight. I want to take you out. You and the kids with me and Lee—Miss Hunt. I want to take you all out to eat at a nice restaurant. You've been so good to me since I've been here, and you work so hard all the time, I just want to do that."

"George," said Exie, "you don't have to spend your money like that. I'll fix up something here. You can ask Miss Hunt to come over and join us if you want to. I don't mind."

He had been afraid she would try something like that.

"No," he said. "No. I want to do this. I want to take everybody out. I've been paid now, and I've been depending on you for long enough. It's time I gave you a little something back. Besides . . ."

He paused. He hadn't really wanted to use the next argument, but he couldn't sense that Exie was softening up any. He didn't know what else to say.

"Besides," he went on, "we've all been kind of—tense, uneasy around the table with Rider gone. A meal out will be a change of pace, help pass the time. Exie, please let me do this. You'll enjoy it, and so will the kids."

Exie looked up at George. She appeared to be just a little exasperated with him.

"All right, George," she said. "We'll go."

"Good," said George, breaking into a wide smile. "Good. Well, I have to go tell Lee. I have to ask her to go with us. I think she will. I'll get her and then I'll come back up here for you all and then we'll go. I'll be back later."

Tootie and Buster were all dressed up and ready to go. They were waiting in the dog run, using all their willpower to keep from running and playing and messing up their fine going-out clothes. Exie was still in the house. When they heard the horses coming up the road, they couldn't be still any longer. They ran out into the road to watch. It was a beautiful, shining surrey pulled by two white horses. The surrey was painted a bright red, and it had a black cloth top with red fringe around the edges. The children's eyes opened wide as they watched the beautiful vehicle approach. When it got close enough for them to recognize the driver, they began to shout.

"*Jaji, Jaji.*"

George stopped the surrey in the road just there by the dog run. "Whoa. Whoa," he said.

"We going to ride in this?" asked Tootie.

"Yes, we are," said George, climbing down out of the front seat.

"Where we going?" asked Buster.

"We're going to get Miss Hunt," said George, "and then we're all going down to the Tahlequah House to eat dinner."

"Tahlequah House," said Tootie. "That's fancy."

"Let's go then," shouted Buster. "We're ready."

"We been ready for a long time," said Tootie.

"We'll go in just a minute," said George. "I'll go get your mother."

Just then Exie came outside. She was dressed up for the occasion, and George, who had always thought that she was a handsome woman, was struck by her beauty. Rider was certainly a lucky man, he thought, to have such a family. Then a darker thought crossed his mind. He wondered where Rider was and what he was doing. Then he told himself once again that Go-Ahead Rider could take care of himself. There was nothing to worry about.

"You sure do look lovely, Exie," he said.

"Thank you, George."

George helped Exie and the kids into the surrey, then climbed up himself. He took the reins and gave them a snap, and the surrey took off with a sudden lurch forward. They would have a grand time. George would be doing something nice for Rider's family. He would be giving them a little back for all they had done for him. At the same time he would be courting Lee. He felt great. The only thing missing for it to be a perfect evening was Rider.

Chapter Sixteen

Rider and Lovely were waiting outside the Pioneer Boarding Car as Mulford came back outside. He stepped heavily down the stairs and trudged over to the other two men.

"He's gone," he said. "Checked out."

"What now?" said Lovely.

"My bet is he'll try to catch a train out of here," said Rider. "I'm going to the station and watch for him."

"He could get out of town by train or by stage," said Mulford.

"Or horseback," said Lovely.

"That means we need to cover the stage station, the railroad depot, and the livery stables," said Mulford. "I think I can round up enough men to do that. Rider, like you said, you go on to the depot. Woody, why don't you take the stage station. I'll get some men together as quick as I can and send them out to watch the liveries. If he's still in town, we'll find him."

Beehunter tied his horse to a hitchrail in front of a large department store. He could tell what kind of an establishment it was, but he couldn't read the signs. As he stepped up onto the sidewalk, a man walking past spoke to him. Beehunter didn't know what the man said, but it seemed friendly. He nodded and smiled, and the man went on. He wondered where Rider might be. Muskogee was a big town. He had hoped that he would overtake Rider somewhere on the trail, before Rider had a chance to get lost in this city. Now he didn't know where to begin. He probably couldn't even talk to the Indians in this town. They were Creeks. He didn't know their language, only his own Cherokee. He was absolutely alone, and his task seemed almost hopeless. He walked up to the storefront, turned around, and leaned back against the building. He stood and watched the people rushing past, going in all directions at once. He wondered where anyone could be going in such a hurry. Then he saw Lyons. He was sure the man hadn't seen him. Lyons was on the other side of the street, hurrying along like all the rest of the people in this town. He was carrying a suitcase in his left hand, and he had a large revolver hanging at his right side. Beehunter pulled his hat down low in front of his face, ducked his head, and started to follow Lyons. Rider had come to Muskogee after this man. If he kept his eye on Lyons, sooner or later he would find Rider.

Rider waited at the depot. He stayed on the opposite side of the street, hoping that he would catch sight of Lyons trying to buy his ticket without allowing Lyons the chance of seeing him. He knew that he might be spotted by Lyons, but that would be better than allowing Lyons to get away undetected. He filled his pipe and smoked it and watched. And he thought about his family back in Tahlequah. He missed them. He knew that he wasn't terribly far away and he hadn't been gone all that long. But he missed them.

He wasn't worried about them. Not exactly. Not really. George would watch out for them. He knew that. But he did miss them.

And he wondered how George was handling things on his own. He expected that George would do just fine. Perhaps they would go ahead and appoint George sheriff. If they were smart, he thought, they would do that. After all, Rider had resigned, and they needed to fill his position. They wouldn't find a better man for it. And usually it was a pretty good job. Tahlequah was a quiet town most of the time. Not like this railroad town called Muskogee. He felt a sense of pride and accomplishment when he realized that his National Council had defeated the railroad interests and that Tahlequah would not become another railroad town like Muskogee. He drew at his pipe, but it had gone out. He tapped the pipe against the bottom of his left boot and tucked it back into his pocket. People were beginning to go into the depot in groups, in more numbers. It must be getting near arrival time for the next train, he thought. They must be going in to get their tickets. Many of them carried bags. He watched closely, hoping to catch sight of Lyons.

Lyons stopped.

"Damn," he said out loud but in a low, harsh whisper. "Damn him."

He had been heading for the depot, intending to buy a ticket on the next train south, his destination Texas. The train would be pulling in soon, and he wanted to be on it, but there was that damned Rider. He was just standing there, watching. Lyons gripped the handle of his new Smith and Wesson Russian. He squeezed the handle and he gritted his teeth. He ached to put a bullet in Rider, several bullets, but he could not make himself pull the gun. Was he a coward? Of course not, he told himself. It was broad daylight, and there were way too many people around. He would never be able to get away with it. Not now. Not here. Perhaps there would be another time. He loosened his grip on the Russian, and then he realized how tightly he was clenching his teeth. His jaw was sore already from the tension. He stood for a moment and took a few deep breaths, forcing himself to relax at least a little. Well, he would try the stage. It was a change in plans, but it was a way out of town, a way away from Rider. He would try the stage.

Beehunter saw Lyons stop, saw him grip his revolver, then saw him turn and leave. From where he stood, Beehunter could not see what Lyons was looking at. He did not know that Rider was up ahead, did not know where Lyons was going. He did know that he didn't want to be seen by Lyons or to lose sight of Lyons, so when Lyons turned to retrace his own steps, Beehunter faded down a side street and waited until Lyons had passed him by, then he resumed following him. Near the stage station, Lyons spotted Lovely. Then he began to figure out the situation he was in.

Lovely had come from Tahlequah with Rider. Lovely was a federal lawman. That meant that they likely had something on him, something that he was unaware of. It also meant the strong possibility of other lawmen being involved. There was a marshal's office in Muskogee. Lovely would have enlisted help there. The railroad was out and so was the stage. He would have to get a horse. But if they were watching the depot and the stage station, wouldn't they also be watching the livery stables? Of course they would. If that was his next thought, it would almost certainly have been theirs as well. He was trapped. Trapped. And it was only a matter of time before someone would spot him in Muskogee. He could sneak out of town on foot. That was the only way. He suddenly felt very conspicuous carrying his suitcase. He stopped for a moment and leaned against the wall, looking up and down the sidewalk. He set the suitcase down at his feet, took out a handkerchief, and mopped his brow. He saw no one on the street he recognized, nor anyone who appeared to be following him or watching him. He stood up straight and walked down the street, abandoning the suitcase. At the next corner he turned. He was walking east toward Arkansas. He would tackle this problem one step at a time. The first step was to get out of Muskogee.

When Beehunter realized that Lyons was leaving town, he knew that he had a problem. He had not been sent to trail Lyons. He had been sent to find Rider, to help him out if need be. But Rider did not seem to be anywhere around, in spite of the fact that it was Lyons Rider had followed in the first place. Could something have happened to Rider? Beehunter didn't know what to do. He could keep following Lyons, but for how long? How far? He could go back to Muskogee and look for Rider. But where? He could also go back to Tahlequah and tell George Tanner that he had failed. That he did not want to do.

He stayed on Lyons's trail a little while longer. He was traveling along a road that was not much more than a wagon trail heading east. He must, Beehunter thought, be going to Arkansas, but he was certainly going to have a long walk. When it became clear to Beehunter that Lyons had nowhere to go but straight ahead, straight east along this road, he turned around and started back toward Muskogee. He still wasn't sure what he would do, but he did know that he had no intention of walking to Arkansas behind Lyons. He would go back to his horse, and then he would decide. If he should decide after all to follow Lyons, at least it would be on horseback. He would be able to catch up easily with Lyons if he decided to do that.

Lyons's pace had slowed considerably. His feet hurt. He could feel blisters that had been raised on his feet by his long walk, the longest walk he had taken in years. His muscles were beginning to ache as well, and his clothing was soaked with sweat. He stopped to rest and stood panting. He pulled the handkerchief out of his pocket to mop his brow. The handkerchief was still wet from the last mopping. Things had certainly not turned out the way he had planned them. Yes, he had money in his pocket, but there was little he could do with it walking along this wretched little road. He longed for an inn to appear around the next bend in the road. Looking back over his shoulder, he saw no one, heard no telltale sounds. It was quiet and still. Small birds sang in the trees off to the sides of the road. He faced forward again and forced his tired legs and sore feet to carry him along his way. He walked another fifty feet or so to make it around the next curve, and then he stopped again. There was a house. It was a small house, probably the house of a small subsistence farmer, he thought. It was no inn, but it would do. It would have to do. He hurried toward the house, but before he reached it, a man stepped out through the front door and stood on the porch, holding in his hands a shotgun. Lyons stopped. He took a deep breath, and then he smiled.

"Hello," he said. "Might I get a drink of water from you?"

"Water's cheap," said the man. "Help yourself."

He jerked his head toward a barrel that stood on the right-hand side of the porch. As Lyons moved forward toward the barrel, the man moved to his own left, keeping a careful eye on Lyons, holding the shotgun ready. Lyons noticed that the man took a good long look at his Russian pistol. A dipper hung on a nail on the post beside the barrel. Lyons took it down and dipped it into the water barrel. He took a long drink, and it felt good.

"Mind if I sit a spell?" he said. "I just walked out from Muskogee."

"A long walk," said the man. "Go ahead and set."

Lyons sat down on the edge of the porch with a groan.

"Say," he said, "you wouldn't have a drink of whiskey around the place, would you?"

The man didn't answer.

"I can pay," said Lyons. He reached into an inside coat pocket, slowly and carefully because of the shotgun, and he extracted from the pocket a wallet. Opening the wallet he pulled out a bill.

"Yeah," said the man. "I might have."

Elwood Lovely was getting bored. The stagecoach was about ready to load up and pull out on its way to Fort Gibson, and he had seen no sign of Omer Lyons. He hadn't really expected to. Fort Gibson was back in the direction of Tahlequah, and Lyons would have little reason to head back that way. If he had no other means of getting out of town, away from Rider, he might take the coach. But Lovely doubted it very much. He rolled a cigarette and lit it, and as he tossed the match away he noticed a familiar figure walking down the street. He looked again to be sure.

"Beehunter," he shouted.

One of the few English words that Beehunter might have understood was the translation of his own name, but he was not attuned to the sounds of language in Muskogee. Expecting to hear nothing but English and Creek, Beehunter simply was not listening to the voices around him. He kept on walking. Lovely looked after Beehunter. He looked back at the stagecoach. The passengers were climbing aboard. He made a move as if to follow Beehunter, then hesitated. Lyons might come along at the last minute and get on the coach. Get it rolling, he said to himself. Come on. One more passenger got into the coach. The driver shut the door and climbed up onto the box. He released the brake and snapped the reins, and the stagecoach jerked forward and started to roll down the street. Lovely ran after Beehunter. Coming up beside him, he put a hand on Beehunter's shoulder.

"Beehunter," he said. "Wait up."

Beehunter recognized Lovely, but he didn't understand what the man was saying.

"What the hell are you doing here?" said Lovely

Beehunter responded in Cherokee. Lovely looked around in frustration as if he might just see someone around who could translate for him. He knew, of course, that the Indians in Muskogee were mostly Creek. Finally he gestured for Beehunter to follow him, and Beehunter understood the makeshift sign language. Lovely led him to the railroad depot and Rider, who was still watching the station. The train had not yet arrived.

"Hey, Rider," shouted Lovely. "Look who I found."

Looking surprised, Rider spoke in Cherokee to his Cherokee friend.

"Beehunter," he said, "what are you doing in Muskogee?"

"I came looking for you," said Beehunter, "in case you need some help."

"I'm here unofficially," said Rider. "I can't hire a deputy here."

"I'm unofficial, too," said Beehunter. "You came after Lyons?"

"Yes."

"I saw him."

"When?" said Rider.

"I just came from him. I can show you. He left town."

Lyons had another drink of the rotgut the farmer had brought out of his house. He would have liked more, but he knew that he should be getting along. His feet were sore, and he didn't like the idea of starting to walk again. He had noticed a small barn out behind the house.

"You have a horse around here?" he asked. "A saddle horse?"

"I just got one," said the man, "and I need her."

"I'd pay you a good price," said Lyons.

The farmer was a good horse trader, and his skill was enhanced by the fact that he held a shotgun in his hands. Pretty soon Lyons had agreed to a price way too high. He was angry, but he was also desperate and in a hurry.

"Wait here," said the farmer. "I'll fetch her out."

Lyons had another drink of the man's whiskey while he waited. Then the farmer came walking back from the barn. He was leading a brown mare by the reins. The horse had on a homemade hack-amore but no saddle.

"Where's the saddle?" said Lyons.

"You didn't buy the saddle."

"Well, you got one?"

"I got one."

"I figured you'd let me have the saddle with the horse," said Lyons.

"You'll have to pay extra."

Lyons got up and walked to the horse. As he approached, the man dropped the reins and backed away. Lyons caught up the reins and moved to the horse's left side.

"To hell with you," he said. "I'll ride her bareback."

He made two false starts at mounting, then stood with his arms resting on the animal's back.

"Oh, hell," he said. "All right. Go get me the saddle."

"Let's see your money first."

Lyons took out his wallet again. He pulled out a few bills. The man didn't budge. He pulled out another. The farmer stepped forward just enough to reach out and take the money.

"Be right back," he said.

When the farmer walked toward his barn, he left Lyons standing in the yard on the far side of the mare. Lyons felt his heartbeat increase. He slipped the big Smith and Wesson out of its holster and waited. The farmer came back carrying the saddle. He still held the shotgun, too, but it was not in a ready position. The saddle had him off guard. The man was within ten feet of the mare when Lyons raised the revolver up and laid his arm across the horse's back. The man stopped. His mouth fell open and his eyes opened wide. He dropped the saddle, intending to swing his shotgun around, but before the saddle hit the ground, Lyons had pulled the trigger. The heavy .44 Russian slug smashed into the man's sternum and tore apart his backbone on the way out. His face sagged and took on a stupid expression. He walked backward two steps, stopped, then dropped to his knees and fell forward. Lyons steadied the horse, and he ran to the body to retrieve his money. Then he saddled the mare and climbed onto her back.

Rider, Beehunter, and Lovely were riding along the road where Beehunter had followed Lyons earlier. Beehunter had assured Rider that they were not far behind the man. They couldn't be, he said. Lyons had been on foot, and he didn't walk very fast. Beehunter had calculated the time it had taken him to walk back to town, find Rider, get their horses, and then ride out along the road. Lyons was not far ahead. Then they heard the shot.

"Let's go," said Rider. They spurred their horses into a run. Rounding a bend in the road, they came to the farmhouse. Lovely spotted the body first. The three riders slowed almost to a stop.

"Go on," said Lovely. "I'll see about this."

Rider and Beehunter rode on while Lovely dismounted and ran to where the unfortunate farmer lay. He soon saw that the man was dead, and he remounted his horse. Then he rode hard after his two companions.

Omer Lyons heard the riders coming up behind him. He looked over his shoulder, but he could not see them. In a panic he kicked the sides of his mare and she jumped forward. He rode hard around another curve in the narrow road, and then he saw the outcropping of rocks off to the left side of the road. He turned the mare toward the rocks and pulled her up hard at the base of the outcropping. The horse had not quite stopped when he swung down too hastily from the saddle. He fell to the ground. Scampering to his feet he ran to the rocks and clambered upward. The rocks didn't rise very high, perhaps fifteen feet, but at the top of the rock shelf was an oval-shaped rock. He worked his way behind it and found it to be near perfect. He could settle himself behind it and fire over its top, and he had a good view of the road. He pulled out the big pistol and reloaded the empty chamber. Then he saw them. He took aim and fired.

"Ow. God damn," Lovely cried, grabbing at his left shoulder. He half fell, half threw himself from the saddle. His companions each quickly dismounted, taking hold of him and helping him to the side of the road. They got themselves back into the trees that grew beside the road. Beehunter pulled a bandanna out of his hip pocket and wrapped Lovely's wound as best he could.

"He's up there on those rocks," said Rider.

"What the hell's he shooting?" said Lovely.

Rider eased around the tree, which was protecting him, and fired a shot at the rocks. Lyons came up and shot again just as Rider ducked back behind the tree. The .44 Russian bullet tore bark from the tree just about where Rider had been.

"It's a pistol," said Rider.

"Damn heavy load," said Lovely. "That's a big gun."

"I'm going to try to work my way closer through these trees," said Rider. "You just stay put."

Then he turned to Beehunter and spoke in Cherokee.

"Stay with him," he said. "I'm going closer."

Beehunter also realized that Lyons was firing no ordinary pistol. It was too accurate at that range, and it made a powerful loud noise. He knew why Rider was creeping through the woods to get closer. His Colts were no match for that thing at their present distance. As Rider vanished through the woods, Beehunter looked out onto the road. The three abandoned horses were milling around nervously and snorting. Then from somewhere up ahead Rider fired a shot at Lyons. Lyons soon figured out that someone had crept closer, and he shifted his position on the rocks to compensate for the different angle. Rider fired again, and Lyons popped up from behind his cover to aim the big Russian model revolver. Beehunter ran onto the road to the side of his horse and pulled his Henry rifle out of its scabbard. He took quick but careful aim and pulled the trigger. The .44 rifle slug struck Lyons just above the right eye and tore out a piece of the back of his skull. His head jerked backward with the impact, his hands went limp, and he dropped his pistol, finally toppling back off the rocks.

Chapter Seventeen

"We had to leave Woody back in Muskogee," Rider was saying. "He's hurting some, but he'll be all right, I think. Anyhow, it's over."

He walked over to the coffeepot on the stove in the sheriff's office. Then he shot a glance at George.

"Can I have some of this?" he said.

"Sure," said George.

"Well, since it all happened outside of our jurisdiction," said Judge Boley, who was seated on the edge of the big desk, "it'll be up to the federal lawmen to write up the reports, tie up all the loose ends. At any rate, we're glad you're back."

Boley reached down to pick up Rider's badge, which was still on top of the desk where Rider had dropped it days ago.

"Go-Ahead."

Rider looked at the judge just in time. Boley pitched the star at him from across the room. Rider had a cup in his right hand, but he managed to catch the flying badge with his left.

"Now that you're back home you'd better pin that back on," said Boley.

"I resigned," said Rider.

"I didn't accept your resignation. You didn't write it out."

"You want me to write it out?" asked Rider.

"Write what out?" said Boley. "I don't know what you're talking about. See you around."

The judge picked up his hat and walked out of the office without another word. Rider put his cup on top of the stove and pinned the badge back on. He hadn't expected that from Boley, but he was glad. He did like his job. He looked at George.

"Well," he said, "everything been all right around here?"

"Yeah," said George. "No problems. I'm getting married."

"Yeah?"

"I asked her last night, and she said yes."

Rider took a sip of his coffee.

"You talking about Miss Hunt, I guess," he said.

"Sure," said George. "Who else?"

"I just thought I should ask. You never know. Well, that's real good, George. I'm glad for you. Congratulations."

"Thank you, Rider."

"George?"

"Yeah?"

"You ain't moved in with her yet, have you?"

"No," said George, his voice indignant. "We're not married yet. You're going to be the best man. You will, won't you?"

"I'd be proud. But right now, since you're still living at my house, let's go home. I want to see my family."

George looked at Rider. It was sure good to have him back. Everything had worked out for the best. He thought about Exie and Tootie and Buster up on the bluff waiting for Rider to come home and wondering about him, and he thought that he didn't really need to be in the way just then.

"You go on, Rider," he said. "I've got some paperwork to catch up on here. I'll lock things up, and I'll be along later. Okay?"